LOYALTY

POE DOUGH

Editor: Stacey M. Robinson

Cover Designer: Chamika Dinesh

Layout Designer: Istvan Szabo, Ifj. - Sapphire Guardian International / Fiverr

Publisher: POE UP! PUBLISHING (CLEVELAND, OHIO)

ISBN-13: 978-0-578-81492-6

Library of Congress Control Number: 9780578814926

For more information regarding publicity or author interviews, please email Poe Dough at porcshedough@gmail.com.

TABLE OF CONTENTS

Chapter 1:

Tuff-Chilli

Loyalty rushed to get to work—it was her first day at the Justice Center in Downtown Cleveland. Jumping out of bed while realizing the time, she speed-walked to the closet, wiping the sleep out of her eyes. Loyalty scammed through to find clothes that were specific to wear just for today.

Instantly annoyed as she moved hangers, the phone rang.

"Hello?" Brittany, said, sounding half asleep

"Why didn't you take the clothes to the cleaners?" Loyalty responded, speaking firmly into the phone.

"Save all the drama, please," Brittany, said, in a nasty tone.

"Girl, bye. You are the assistant; it's your job," Loyalty responded while brushing her teeth, pissed at Brittany.

"Don't worry. I'm going now to get the clothes out the cleaners. Chill out." Brittany hung up.

"Selfish as fuck," Loyalty said to herself, slamming the phone down on the bathroom counter.

Walking back over to the closet to find something else to wear, Loyalty looked at the selection of clothes: Balenciaga, Fendi, Chanel, and Gucci. She was frustrated, sitting on the floor of the closet, with her legs folded, confused, and her hands covering her head. She was sitting in so much inner pain...not really because of the dry cleaning, but really just the loneliness she had to endure.

Loyalty wiped small tear drops from her lashed eyes, getting up from the furry twenty-five-hundred-dollar purple rug in the closet, peeking out only to look at the time. It was already eight a.m., and work began at nine a.m. Jogging

1

over to her phone laying on her canopy bed, Loyalty sent Brittany a quick text: *I love you. Sorry, sis.*

Loyalty placed the phone down to take a shower, rushing since she didn't want to risk being late for work.

Dressed in a Fashion Nova pencil skirt and matching blouse (courtesy of Balenciaga), Loyalty put on shoes to give that extra look—looking into the vanity mirror instantly made her feel better. She programmed the alarm to the house and walked to the 445 BMW in the garage. Turning the radio station to some smooth jazz, she hoped it would calm her thoughts so she could focus more on her daily tasks.

Loyalty entered the doors of the Justice Center dressed like a million bucks, although she really felt like a penny. Walking into the conference room of fifteen people, she smiled.

"How is everyone doing?" Loyalty spoke with so much passion for her work, greeting all the staff.

"We are doing well, thank you," everyone responded at their own pace before detective Tracey Martinez began speaking about recent federal cases. The meeting carried on for hours—at least five—and when work was finally over, Loyalty's stomach started rumbling terribly.

The best part about leaving work in the inner city is seeing couples holding hands on the busy streets, Loyalty thought to herself on the way walking to Zoup Restaurant, located on 4th Street in Cleveland, Ohio. She didn't need any samples—Loyalty ordered the same items off the menu that she always ordered.

"Yes, the Cheddar Broccoli Bowl and Chicken Toscana," Loyalty spoke softly to the cashier.

"Anything else for you?" the cashier asked.

"That's it, Love," Loyalty spoke with a wide smile.

"OK, your total is twenty-ninety-five."

After a few minutes passed, Loyalty grabbed her food and walked over to the window to sit and finish watching the busy city of Cleveland rotate.

* * *

Grandma Joy kept me active, Brittany thought to herself. She dropped out of school at sixteen years old and looked at things far different than Loyalty did. Loyalty was very smart, and always put education first. Loyalty acted better that she did—more important. Loyalty was the reason why new employment was needed. To find something that fit Brittany's lifestyle.

She bumped into a great guy at The Alibi Night Club that he owned, the night before. Word around town was that he may be a drug dealer, but it was Brittany's first time seeing him in the club. Cream was a catch, and Brittany realized that she needed to play ball. She got out the iPhone to listen to some music as she started to clean the apartment.

"Damn!" Brittany yelled to herself. "I have to call Grandma Joy. Fucking forgot," she ranted. Grandma Joy was sixty years old, struggling with minor heart problems. She had taken Brittany and Loyalty in to care for them, as young children at the time. Their mom and dad left them both and never returned.

Grandma was the rock for me, Brittany thought as the phone rang. *Loyalty kept us strong through it all.*

"Hey, Baby," Grandma Joy answered with her raspy voice.

"Hi, Mama Joy, checking on you," Brittany responded, smiling like a kid on the phone. "Are you doing OK?"

"Baby, doing much better today. How is your sister?" Grandma Joy responded while covering up in her robe. Coughing.

"Loyalty is OK." Brittany was thrown off by Grandma Joy's question.

"Brittany, Baby. You and Loyalty just love one another, OK?" Grandma Joy pleaded gently, asking Brittany.

Brittany was annoyed. "OK, Grandma Joy. Love you! Be over later tomorrow," she said. After hanging up, Brittany rolled her eyes. She always felt like a shadow to Loyalty. Brittany had enough.

* * *

Loyalty arrived home from work, pulling into the two-car garage of her teal colored three-bedroom home in WestLake village at the Colony. She was irritated. Single now for a few years, Loyalty had given up the local bars and churches long ago. College was the best option for Loyalty to be able to remain successful, and she was proud to say that part was over.

She felt her loneliness as she entered the house, thinking to herself, *walking inside the house sends my emotions through the roof.* She rushed over and poured a glass of wine at the kitchen table. Sitting at the table sipping wine, thoughts ran through her mind—she realized how important Brittany was to her. Brittany was smart and talented with a rare sexy look: full breasts and a big bottom. She made Brittany an assistant to help with bills and hoped that it remained a positive lifestyle for herself.

Looking through her phone, she continued to feel anxious, remembering that she hadn't called to check on Grandma Joy in about a week. She placed the glass in the sink. *Grandma joy always knew when something wasn't right with her Loyalty,* Loyalty told herself while scanning through her iPhone. Grandma Joy's intentions were always pure; Loyalty was incredibly grateful.

Chapter 2:

EXAGGERATION

Loyalty was laying down in Chanel's bed, looking up to the ceiling, happy Chanel was in her life. She often expressed these sincere feelings to Chanel, who always brought laughter and motivation to her life, extremely. Chanel was a great friend and had always been like a little sister. They met in college and had been very close ever since.

"Can you hurry up? I'm lonely out here," Loyalty yelled at Chanel, who was showering.

"OK, Girl," Chanel yelled back, while cutting off the water. Chanel entered the room ass hole naked.

"Chanel?" Loyalty spoke while giggling.

"All this beauty is beautiful," Chanel said while twerking, laughing. Loyalty picked up a magazine to read, shaking her head.

"Wasup? Why are you looking sad?" Chanel asked her friend, in a positive tone.

"Money is not everything; it is something," Loyalty replied while flipping the pages of the urban magazine.

"I love you. Let's go shopping at Great Northern Mall," Chanel responded, flipping her hair. Jumping up and down on the bed, Chanel tried her best to cheer Loyalty up.

Loyalty gently lifted up from the pillows with ease. "Food and clothes on me," Loyalty responded.

"Look at you, splurging on your girl," Chanel said, smiling while hitting Loyalty with a pillow.

"I love you, crazy girl," Loyalty laughed. "Get dressed. I have to meet up with Brittany for dinner later tonight."

* * *

Brittany is on her way to cook salmon and rice. *Brittany could cook her ass off,* Loyalty thought. Loyalty was a terrible cook and thought about the time she was cooking food for Grandma Joy and the kitchen was left literally burnt in flames. Thinking about it made Loyalty laugh, as she cleaned the kitchen before Brittany arrived.

"Hey, Siri? Play NBA Youngboy, No Mention," Loyalty yelled at the stereo as she wiped off the table. There was light outside on a nice summer day; Loyalty walked over to unlock the door to let some great air come inside.

The doorbell rang, and Brittany stood at the door wearing a Chanel black jumpsuit and brown suede ankle boots. "Hey sis," Brittany spoke to Loyalty, reaching out for a hug.

"Hey, Babe," Loyalty hugged Brittany, and she brought the food to the counter. "I decorated the table, and everything should be set up for us," Loyalty explained, walking back to the kitchen.

"OK, turn the music down a bit, my head is throbbing," Brittany told Loyalty while washing her hands to begin the quick meal. "Loud-ass stereo," Brittany said looking over at Loyalty.

"Guess so," Loyalty responded, rolling her eyes. "Siri, turn the volume down."

Loyalty sat at the table, bored on Facebook until the food was finished. Scrolling down Facebook, she realized she just didn't care much about single life anymore. Loyalty thought deeply while on the phone looking at a couple's memes and photos.

"Food be finished in a few," Brittany spoke softly, but aggressively.

Placing the phone on the table, Loyalty went over to the cabinets to get plates and wine glasses for mimosas during dinner to help finish setting up. Brittany made plates, then sat in a chair with a napkin and silverware in front of her on the marble glass table. Shortly after beginning the meal, Loyalty just felt a bit of tension—she knew something was weird with Brittany, but just didn't know exactly what.

They both ate their meals.

"Hey, stay over and watch *Golden Girls?*" Loyalty asked Brittany genuinely.

"Yeah, that's cool," Brittany said, looking up at Loyalty finishing the rest of her food.

"Great!" Loyalty was excited and rushed to the hall closet. "Here go some pajamas, a towel, and wash cloth." She handed Brittany a few overnight things, where she sat on the couch. "And thanks for being here. You are also a very good cook...impressively good," Loyalty told Brittany as the *Golden Girls* continued.

Ten minutes later, Loyalty was asleep.

The next morning, Brittany had already left without even saying goodbye. Loyalty walked over to the black blinds to gaze out the window and witness the sun and birds chirping outside the windows.

Well hopefully the dry cleaning comes on time today from Brittany, Loyalty thought to herself. *I have a busy week ahead...it better come, or Brittany not getting a paycheck.* Loyalty walked over to the bathroom to brush her teeth and ran some quick shower water to get to work for 9:00am. The time was 8:10am.

Twenty-five minutes later, Loyalty was dressed and, on the way, out the door, headed to her 445 BMW.

So many men admired Loyalty at the job due to her sassiness, confidence, and work ethic. She spent several hours managing cases until she was finally off work. Then, she walked over to Zoup restaurant to eat her favorite bowl of soup.

The Zoup cashier smiled. "Hi there," she said, speaking with enthusiasm. "Coming to get the regular? Broccoli Cheddar..."

"Yes, Sweetheart. Just pack it to go, I'm not dining today, thanks," Loyalty said as she stood at the register with grace and patience.

"No problem. The total is nine bucks," the cashier said. Loyalty politely handed her credit card over.

"Get out the damn way!" Loyalty yelled as she waved her hand, on the way home, avoiding traffic. "Now why would you break so hard?" Loyalty spoke as she turned the volume down to the soft jazz she was listening to. Minutes later, she was headed to the gate of her community and punched the code to enter. The gates opened. Pulling in the driveway, exhausted, was ready to take a nap at any moment.

Unlocking the house alarm, Loyalty placed her briefcase at the side of the door, went over to the fridge to pour a cold glass of mimosa, headed over to the shower down the hall, and turned the steamy water on. In the bathroom, she glanced into the mirror as the fog started to appear and faded her reflection away. Loyalty unwrapped her bun ponytail and sat thinking and dreaming of the future husband she craved.

"I just want somebody, not just anybody," Loyalty spoke out loud, leaving the bathroom as the water still ran.

Her phone rang.

"Hello, did you call Grandma Joy today?" Brittany asked.

"Hey, nope. Maybe by later on, to visit her though," Loyalty stated while sipping another taste of her sweet red wine.

"OK, see you there," Brittney agreed to meet her sister. Loyalty ended the call, walked back in the bathroom, undressed, and then sat in the tub to manifest.

Grandma Joy meant so much to Loyalty, but she had not managed to call lately because she had been so busy. Loyalty splashed some water up to her face, remembering the day she purchased Grandma Joy's first home. *Man was Mama excited,* Loyalty smiled to herself. Every month Grandma Joy's bills were paid because of Loyalty. *Shit, she raised this intelligent paralegal,* Loyalty thought. She honestly believed Grandma Joy deserved it all.

Loyalty—finally done with soaking and relaxing—threw on some clothes and headed to Grandma Joy's house although she was very tired. *Oh well,* she thought, deciding to stop at a nearby Target first. Loyalty browsed the blanket section, deciding to pick up a colorful quilt for her Grandma, and a couple of kitchen appliances. The line was extremely long, and Loyalty became impatient. A few minutes later, she pulled up to Grandma Joy's house only a few miles from the store. Loyalty felt good about Brittany not being there yet, because she just wanted to bond with Grandma Joy. She knocked on the door anxiously.

"Hey, Mama Joy!" Loyalty said, while giving her grandma a huge hug.

"Hey, Baby, thought something happened to you," Grandma Joy said, staring right into Loyalty's eyes.

"I've been OK, just busy, Grandma. A few things for you," she said. Loyalty walked into the house and sat on the couch to show grandma her gifts, talking in an African accent, jokingly.

"Thought that was some liquor!" Grandma Joy stated sarcastically, with her hands on her hips.

Loyalty burst out laughing at Grandma Joy. "Nope, sure don't."

There was a knock on the door. "This Brittany!" She kept knocking.

"Sup, Baby Sis?" Loyalty greeted Brittany at the door.

"Hey, Family!" Brittany said, entering the home.

Grandma Joy smiled. "You both take a seat at the kitchen table—let me heat up some of this food, oxtails, greens, fried chicken with fried tomatoes."

"Appreciate you, Grandma," Brittany explained, wiping off the table and then looking over at Loyalty, giving her a slight dirty look. Loyalty paid no attention to her, and instead stayed on her phone and navigated her laptop.

Listening to old stories that Grandma Joy told, they all laughed (and almost cried) from the memories, avoiding the talk about their mother and father who left their girls to basically starve to death. Their dad was a drug addict who was never ever home.

Loyalty started to think of the time that Brittany and her were walking home from school and caught their dad in front of this strange building on Benham. She knew, even at the age eleven, that those people were not good people. Loyalty was super smart and remained knowing that her dad was a damaged good.

After a few hours passed, Loyalty became sleepy. "OK, Grandma, about to head home now. Brittany, leaving now," she said, reaching over to kiss her grandma. "I love you," she said in a sad tone, and then left immediately.

CHAPTER 3:

CREME POT

Loyalty woke up thinking to herself, *Friday my day, a total of eighty hours this week was home; I can sleep all day,* until the phone rang. "Hello?"

"Hi, is this Ms. Monroe?"

Loyalty replied, "Yes. This is Ms. Monroe."

"My name is Miranda. I am calling due to you signing up for a fraud alert, and we've suspected some unusual activity with your account."

"Wow. How much was suspected to be missing from the account?" Loyalty replied.

"Two-thousand dollars, Ms. Monroe," Miranda replied.

Loyalty was fucking livid! She looked at the phone, threw it at the wall, and couldn't control the pissed off feeling taking over her. *The dirty bitch stole from me, bought herself a car, and I gave the bitch a job,* she thought to herself as she jumped out of bed and walked to the kitchen to pour herself a cold glass of wine.

Loyalty was now heated and pissed, and drinking was not making the situation any better. Upon swallowing the last of the drink, and rushing into the shower, she thought, *Today was supposed to be a good day,* as she washed her face.

"How could Brittany?" Loyalty said out loud, shaking head in utter disbelief' as she finished showering, and looked inside her custom gold drawers, pulling out a purple Champion jogging suit. She threw on clothes, socks, and Balenciaga tennis shoes. Grabbing curly hair to put into a ponytail, after picking up her car keys, Loyalty set the alarm and then left out the door.

Brittany's condo was in Tremont, downtown Cleveland, not too far from Loyalty's house. Loyalty was getting closer to Brittany home, with negative thoughts coming across her mind. She simply chose not to call or text her sister. It was yet another nice day outside, and she hated that this was all happening on her day off. Loyalty pulled up—not even completely parked—and got out the car, furious at the entire situation. She rang the doorbell over and over, seeing that Brittany's car was parked in the front. As soon as she opened the door, Loyalty yelled at her, starting to become very impatient until she just decided to leave to go over to a bar called the Punchbowl to grab a bite to eat.

Valet took Loyalty's car, and Loyalty walked in to have a seat.

"Hi, my name is Rose; I will be delighted to serve you today," the server said. "Let's start you off with a beverage?"

"Yes, please," Loyalty said, examining the menu. "Let me have the watermelon polo bowl and lobster bacon fries, and a side order of traditional wings with the sweet cilantro sauce. That will be all."

"OK, your order will be here shortly," Rose said.

Loyalty looked down at her watch to discover that it was after twelve p.m. She didn't realize time had passed by so quick! Loyalty was eating food and enjoying the drink ordered and became unsure if she was ready to just enjoy the rest of the day or go home.

Loyalty finished the rest of the food and drink, paid for the meal, and started heading outside to thank and pay the valet to get the car. Loyalty sat in the car, a bit buzzed from the beverage, thinking about how she wanted more drinks.

Driving off to The Alibi Night Club, she decided that she needed some fresh air and flashing lights to get rid of the dark cloud over her. Loyalty was still upset about Brittany. Alibi was about ten minutes away from the Punch Bowl.

Beep, beep. "Come on!" Loyalty yelled. It was going on three p.m. and there were cars parked, but she figured it was cool because she did not want to be bothered with too many people anyway. NBA Youngboy was blasting around her; Loyalty took a seat at the bar. "Yes, double-double shot of Hennessey," Loyalty asked some nice-looking lady behind the bar, who was about five-foot-five with pretty brown skin and looked around the early twenties mark.

The atmosphere smelled like money, liquor, and a dancer entertaining at the time. The dancer was short, and thick, with a bob cut hairstyle, dressed in pink and white, and wearing Louboutin shoes. Loyalty looked over and saw a fine six-foot-one caramel skin toned guy with pretty teeth.

A bartender approached Loyalty. "Excuse me ma'am. The fine gentleman in VIP wanted you to have this." Loyalty looked down and saw that it was four-hundred dollars and a Moet bottle, and one of the bills had his phone number on it. Loyalty accepted his offer, looking over smiling at him. A few more drinks later, the time was past six p.m. Loyalty's body was tired and drained.

What a good time, Loyalty thought to herself. *I don't know why this man gave me money in the first place, but I won't think about it too much.*

The bill with the number was placed on the bed, as Loyalty thought about giving him a call. She then changed clothes and climbed into bed to call the lucky guy. While on the phone with him, her phone rang again.

"Hey. This is Loyalty. Is this the guy who left me a huge tip?"

He replied, "What's up beautiful?" in a serious manner tone. He then asked Loyalty, "Would you like company?" Loyalty's heart was pounding hard before even answering this question.

Loyalty replied, "Sure. For a little while."

"Cool. I'll be outside at The Alibi. Text me your address," the guy told Loyalty.

Feeling so nervous, Loyalty got out the bed dancing, quickly changing into a two-piece Fashion Nova outfit, ordered weeks ago. Her phone rang, and she quickly answered.

"Hello," Loyalty said into the phone.

"I'm at the pearly gate. What is the code to open the door?" the sexy guy on the other end of the phone asked.

Just type in two three four seven, and drive over to the address, Loyalty sent him a quick text. The doorbell rang, and Loyalty's heart instantly began to beat faster as she welcomed him in.

"My name is Devin, by the way," he laughed.

"Come in," Loyalty said as she led Devin to the living room's plush purple sofa.

"So, what kind of work do you do, Loyalty?" Devin awkwardly asked.

"Full-time paralegal at the Justice Center in downtown Cleveland. What about you, Devin?" Loyalty asked. "Where do you work?" Loyalty faced Devin with her legs crossed.

"I own The Alibi and a few more businesses around the Cleveland area," Devin said, and put his hand on Loyalty's thigh.

"That is amazing," Loyalty said to Devin, blushing. "My real name is Alsadi; everyone calls me Loyalty."

"Cute," Devin told Loyalty.

CHAPTER 4:

FALLING IN SIN

The next morning, Loyalty woke up excited to meet up with Devin. She got up, stretched, made the bed, and went to the bathroom to take a quick shower and brush her teeth, while turning the knobs for the shower. She undressed and slipped into the shower. Relaxed.

Shortly after, she grabbed her Lacoste towel, dried off, and lathered her entire body in shea butter oil, spraying some Gucci Guilty all over. Loyalty, finally dressed, looked into the closet filled with clothes, looking for her Fashion Nova jeans with her matching grey 'Fuck Haters' top. Looking into the mirror, Loyalty stood just admiring herself.

"Damn. Feel very confident," she said to herself, walking into the kitchen dressed, ready to go. Loyalty opened the cherry cabinet making a glass of mimosa, feeling nervous. It had been so long since she had a guy around. Loyalty drank the whole glass of wine, put the glass in the sink, and grabbed her car keys. She set the alarm and headed out of the house.

Her phone rang. It was Devin. "Hey, Beautiful," Devin said, smiling slightly.

Loyalty replied, "I'm fine."

"OK, Pretty Lady, be there soon."

"Do not have me waiting," she said. Loyalty looked in the mirror to fix her hair to make sure the look was right. *Hoping this goes well,* she thought to herself. Loyalty's heart kept beating very loudly—at least she thought so as she pulled up to Cracker Barrel.

When Loyalty arrived, Devin spotted her, and went to greet her. He opened the car door and looked at Loyalty, helping her out of her car. Going through the glass doors, he opened up every door for her. The server came to take their order: Devin ordered a turkey bacon sandwich, and Loyalty ordered French toast.

Loyalty and Devin shared conversation for almost two and a half hours; they talked about family, taking trips, his interests, and Loyalty's interests. Devin mentioned that he had been single for almost five years while wrapping up with school and helping out his grandmother. Devin claims that he gave everything to his ex, including his heart and his time. His ex was the least bit satisfied with him; Devin explained honestly. Loyalty looked into Devin's eyes—she could see the hurt and pain.

"Let's go see a movie," Devin asked Loyalty after finishing his pancakes and then taking care of the bill. He pulled up a list of movies to watch.

Following Devin to the movie theater, Loyalty turned on Marvin Gaye's *I Want You* on the radio. She loved that song so much, to the point that it was loud. Fifteen minutes arriving at the theater, they picked and chose the movie *The Equalizer*.

Hours passed, and Loyalty looked at Devin as they walked back to the cars. "Can we go back to your place?" Devin asked. "Let me keep you company tonight." She agreed, and he followed her home—twenty minutes later they arrived, and both walked into the house, stuffed.

Devin opened the door for Loyalty, she took off her shoes and he sat on the sofa to roll a blunt.

"Loyalty," Devin bluntly yelled out. "Comfortable here," he said, getting even more comfortable. Loyalty went into the bedroom to change into a pair of Fashion Nova black shorts with a Nautica top. Afterwards, they walked to the kitchen to make some wine. "You are so beautiful," he added. Devin slid Loyalty closer and closer to him.

Devin was very attractive to Loyalty, and she liked that he smelled like new clothes and laundry detergent.

"Loyalty let me make you happy. Be mine," Devin said, looking at Loyalty and smiling. "Give me a chance. Won't disappoint you Loyalty."

Loyalty responded to see what feeling they had right then and there—Loyalty instantly loved this man, and Devin asked Loyalty to believe him.

"Believe what I concur. Let's start this journey together," Devin asked Loyalty, as they were being calm and honest with one another.

"OK, I will be with you, Devin."

He began to rub Loyalty's legs gently and whispered into her ear, "Won't hurt you," he said, pulling Loyalty's shorts down, and revealing Victoria's Secret panties. Devin had strong hands; Loyalty loved it. Devin lay Loyalty down on the couch face down, pulling Loyalty's hair. "You are mine. Don't forget," Devin spoke aggressively.

Loyalty felt so good. Devin was gorgeous, smooth, and smelled so sexy. He was licking on Loyalty's back, and then placed his tongue into her pussy. Loyalty's body was shaking as Devin's dick grew harder. Devin had Loyalty's body in his control. Devin turned Loyalty around, facing him, and kissing on Loyalty's forehead.

Letting Devin know that her pussy was all his, Loyalty moaned louder as Devin was sticking his dick in—she was so wet. Loyalty became numb instantly, and Devin smacking Loyalty's pecan ass made her moan even louder. Devin loved the shit. Honestly. Devin knew exactly how to satisfy her, and thought to himself, *Loyalty will be forever mine.*

Loyalty waking up on Sunday morning next to Devin felt so right, that Loyalty didn't want to be wrong.

"Whatever it takes to make you happy will do," Devin said, speaking to Loyalty, looking directly in her eyes, and then kissing her forehead. Devin explained, "Be loyal and honest, Loyalty."

Moments later, Devin fell asleep, and Loyalty watching Devin fall asleep made her fall asleep.

Devin's phone rang. "What's up, Bruh?" Devin spoke, waking up from his quick nap.

"Where you are, dude?" Devin's big brother Reese was checking on him. Reese helped Devin with all the businesses, and they went through it all together. Nothing—nor anyone—could tear the bond. Malo was Devin and Reese's best friend and was very loyal. Malo was known for shootings, murders, and kidnappings, and they all were stuck like Gorilla Glue.

"At my girl house," Devin replied.

Reese said, sarcastically, "Now you hitting something new now...your girl, huh?"

"Bruh, really feels solid," Devin explained. Devin looked over at Loyalty still asleep.

"Need to speak with you ASAP, so come over when you are done. Love you kid. Be safe," Reese explained to Devin.

"Yup," he said, and then hung up. Devin washed up, kissed his love, Loyalty and headed out the door.

CHAPTER 5:

CAKE

Loyalty's phone rang. "Helloo," Loyalty said, being funny.

"Sis, nine a.m. meeting this morning," Brittany explained to Loyalty.

Loyalty explained, "Getting dressed now. Be there in thirty minutes," Loyalty said, feeling confident. "Brittany, we need to talk later," Loyalty demanded. "Off around five p.m., so you should be on your way to the house, OK?" Loyalty said, sounding very serious.

"OK," Brittany said, nervously.

"Good," Loyalty said after hanging up. Loyalty was leaving out for work and looked in the mailbox. Nothing was there, so Loyalty got in the car and sped off.

Hours passed until Loyalty was finally off work. Loyalty went straight home to meet Brittany and go over the money situation missing from her account. Loyalty was washing some dishes when Brittany pulled up in the driveway. Loyalty went to unlock the door to let Brittany inside the house. Brittany walked in, panicking and feeling a bit nervous. Loyalty was doing dishes.

Loyalty spoke to Brittany. "Take a seat," she said. Loyalty added, thinking that Brittany took two thousand dollars from her, even though Loyalty didn't need the money.

Brittany stood, looking nonchalant. "So, what's up?" Brittany talked in an annoyed tone.

"Anything you want to explain?"

"Nothing much, just work. You?" Brittany asked, looking guilty.

"Glad you asked," Loyalty said, crossing her arms. "There's two thousand dollars missing from my damn account. What is going on?" Loyalty turned around, crossing her arms, and looking into Brittany eyes, ready to smack the makeup off of her face.

"That has nothing to do with me," Brittany responded, playing with her blue acrylic nails.

"OK," Loyalty said. Looking at Brittany made her angry. She couldn't believe she was sitting there lying. Loyalty went to her bedroom to gather some papers and handed them over to Brittany.

"What are these?" Loyalty tossed the papers. Brittany looked over the sheets of paper, confused.

"Bank transactions. Anything looks familiar?" Loyalty demanded answers.

"Girl, didn't take shit. Nothing, Loyalty," Brittany said, giving Loyalty back the papers, and rolling her eyes. Loyalty decided to drop the conversation and went over the weekly work schedule for Brittany to mark down.

Brittany left eventually. Sitting at the table, annoyed, with her hands on her head frustrated, Loyalty realized she no longer trusted Brittany.

One of the other rooms in Loyalty's home had books, two Apple laptops, and a huge stereo. Loyalty called it a comfort room. Placing a Maxwell CD in the stereo (because *This Woman's Worth* by Maxwell was always smooth with his choice of words), Loyalty went in the bathroom, lit some candles, ran some bath water, and walked back into the kitchen and poured a glass of mimosa to enjoy taking her bath.

In the bath, instead of thinking about Brittany's lying ass, Loyalty thought about Devin. Loyalty sat the glass down on the rug, seductively moving her hands down to her pussy, caressing it. Loyalty thought about Devin and what they both shared that beautiful night.

We have so much in common, Loyalty thought. Devin seemed to love making Loyalty feel relaxed. Devin gave Loyalty chills to where her heart beat rapidly. Devin was a smart man and leader; Loyalty examined Devin well. Devin's mother owned and ran a restaurant that he bought for her. His father was in prison. Devin told Loyalty that he had an older brother, but never cared to share the name. Loyalty brought her hands closer to her, feeling the passion.

Loyalty imagined having her new boyfriend, Devin, with her. He meant so much to Loyalty even though it had been only three weeks of getting to know one another.

The phone rang. "Hello?"

Devin said, speaking gently, "Hey, Baby. Miss you," Devin said with a loud background.

"Miss you more," Loyalty said while playing with herself, smiling at his words.

"What are you doing, Loyalty?" Devin asked.

"Playing with myself, wishing you were here right now," Loyalty told him in confidence.

"Oh yeah? On the way then, to give you a better feel," Devin said, laughing, pushing his dick down from rising.

Loyalty had a normal day at work, thinking of Devin. Loyalty loved Devin. "Knock knock, Miss. Monroe do you need any more paperwork from that other case?"

"No. I'm good," Loyalty expressed. "Thanks Travis." Loyalty continued typing on the laptop. Travis was a manager, mentor, and an all-around great guy. Travis had been patient throughout the entire case and process.

Brittany was still on Loyalty's mind, with no good explanation. Brittany lied. *What are Brittany's real intentions?* Loyalty sat contemplating, finishing up last minute paperwork to work on. She filled in more paperwork then left out for the rest of the day.

Before going home, Loyalty stopped at Menchies for some ice cream, and made a vanilla scoop with marshmallows and M&Ms. Loyalty paid the cashier then left to go home.

Her phone rang. "Hey," she said smiling.

"Where are you?" Devin asked, concerned.

"Leaving from work. Menchies," Loyalty said, blushing from ear to ear. "On the way home soon."

"OK. Want to come see you later," Devin asked.

21

"That is fine," Loyalty told him. "I need to drop clothes off at the cleaner's since me and my sister are at odds," she said, feeling sad.

"Baby, what happened?" Devin asked.

"Just a huge misunderstanding," Loyalty told him, eating her ice cream.

"Baby, whatever is bothering you, it will be OK. Here for you," Devin told Loyalty.

Loyalty reassured him. "Of course, Devin."

It was late, around eight p.m., and Loyalty was on the sofa drinking her wine, watching *Love and Hip Hop*, and laughing her ass off at K. Michelle throwing hot wax. "K. is crazy," Loyalty said, laughing to herself as the doorbell rang.

"Opens up, Girl. It's Devin."

Loyalty unlocked the door and reached her arms out to hug him. Devin walked in. "Took you long enough," Loyalty explained to him. "How was your day, Baby?" she asked.

Devin said, "It was cool. I made some money. So, it is always a good day," he said rubbing his hands together.

"Good. Let me give you a massage," Loyalty said, licking her lips, and standing in between Devin's legs.

Loyalty lifted his shirt off, laying him down across the couch. As she was gently rubbing his back, Devin turned around and started kissing her. Loyalty kissed his chest, rubbing Devin's body, slowly moving down towards his dick putting it all in her mouth.

"With all her heart," Devin told Loyalty while her head went back and forth from the feeling of her lips. Loyalty looked at him, as she sucked Devin's big dick. "I love you," Devin said, while still in a maze of satisfaction.

Loyalty looked at him, knowing he was real. They made love over and over the whole night. What was what Loyalty had been missing. Loyalty's body was craving something unforgettable, passionate, and real. Falling asleep holding Devin made Loyalty feel out of this world. Truly amazing.

Waking up to the smell of bacon and pineapples, turning over there was breakfast, a note, and two lilies on a food tray. *How did he get flowers?* Loyalty said to herself, shocked. *Nice of him.* Opening the note, it read: *Good morning, Adorable Lady. Made you breakfast because you're worth me doing that and more. Left for work so give you a call later, Beautiful.*

CHAPTER 6:

BAG LADY

At the office working, Devin was constantly on Loyalty's mind. Loyalty loved every inch of him, looking at a picture they took days ago at Mentor Beach.

"Miss. Monroe, call's on line two," the receptionist told her. Loyalty pushed the button to answer the call.

"Hello?" she said, sounding happy.

"Hey, Baby. Been missing you all day," Devin explained in a smooth tone.

"Missing you more," Loyalty explained, smiling. "Trying to finish up some paperwork here at work."

"Well, love you. Talk to your fine self later," Devin explained.

"I love you," Loyalty expressed to Devin. Loyalty hung up the phone feeling a bit bored with work. Hours had passed, and it was almost time to leave.

Loyalty's phone rang. "Hello?"

"Hey, it's me, Brittany. Let's meet up."

"I know who this is!" Loyalty said, yelling at the phone, instantly getting upset.

"What's up?" Brittany was a bit concerned. "Just want to catch up with you. Haven't seen you in a few weeks," Brittany explained.

"Come on over. Be home in about an hour," Loyalty told Brittany.

"OK, cool," Brittany sounded excited, and hung up.

While she was frying chicken, Loyalty heard Brittany entering the driveway. Not in the mood, Loyalty decided not to have tension—she wanted to enjoy the rest of the day. Loyalty opened up the front door, and Brittany walked to the kitchen area and said, "Have great news." Brittany sat in the kitchen, watching Loyalty fry chicken. Loyalty, not in the mood, turned around to give Brittany a hug. Brittany clapped her hands together. "Got some good news," Brittany repeated.

"What will that be?" Loyalty asked. "You have the money?" Loyalty asked in a funny tone.

Brittany looked at Loyalty, annoyed. "Girl, what money?" Brittany asked Loyalty. Brittany finished explaining, "Am pregnant." Loyalty's hands folded.

"What..."

"I'm three months pregnant," Brittany expressed, smiling. "Found out yesterday."

"Who is this lucky guy?" Loyalty said, sarcastically.

"Me and This guy has been messing around on and off for five months now," Brittany said, looking down at the table, a bit shameful.

"Bye," Loyalty said, not caring at all.

Making a plate of food, Loyalty sat on the sofa to watch some TV. Loyalty was happy for Brittany, she just could not believe Brittany was always hiding things and keeping things a secret. Brittany had access to the accounts and even an extra key to Loyalty's home. The phone rang, disturbing Loyalty's thoughts.

"Hey Dev," she said, sounding better.

"I'm coming over, you home?"

"I am home," she said, smiling through the phone.

"Cool. On the way, Baby," Dev said, speaking calmly.

* * *

"Take off your clothes," Dev spoke softly in Loyalty's ear, laying on top of her. "Loyalty, love every part of your body, you know that?" Devin spoke to Loyalty, staring into her eyes seductively. He slid her pants down to her ankles, and Devin pulled down his denim jeans, pushing his dick in her. She instantly moaned his name, making him harder and harder, feeling her tightness. She was wrapping her short legs around his masculine body, and he was smacking her thighs, loving every inch of her. Looking into Loyalty's eyes, he asked, "You want my baby?" while still stroking her insides gently.

"Yes...yes," she moaned to Devin, totally into the love act. It was mind blowing, even though it had been only two months. Loyalty was feeling something deep within Devin and couldn't deny herself.

Sweat was dripping off Creme's chest onto Loyalty's from the intense love making.

"Follow me?" Devin asked, grabbing both of Loyalty's hand. She followed Devin into the bathroom. The episode continued, feeling like forever. They made love for hours before going back to sleep in the canopy bed.

* * *

The next morning, Devin was in the kitchen making eggs and bacon for Loyalty again. He woke her up to some breakfast. "Baby, ready to eat?" Devin asked gently, caressing Loyalty's hair.

"Better stop before we start another round," she said. Devin and Loyalty laughed. "Seriously, thank you, Babe," she said, kissing his lips.

Loyalty grabbed the food from Devin and sat and watched some TV. Loyalty could not believe this man and how he made her feel: irreplaceable, joyful, and beautiful.

"See you later, My Dear," Devin said, putting on his pants and shoes, going to work. "Text you in a bit." He kissed Loyalty's forehead, before rushing out the door.

Devin left Loyalty's house feeling overwhelmed. *I have to be real with shorty.* Loyalty meant a lot to Devin. *Have to tell her before she finds out the truth.* Loyalty did not know about Devin's so-called baby that was on the way. Devin shook his head, as the phone rang.

"What's up?" he answered, already knowing who it was.

"Hey, Creme," the woman spoke with excitement in her voice.

"So, you sure that this baby is mine, right?" Devin spoke seriously.

"Are you fucking serious, Dude," she changed her tone.

"You heard me, Brittany. If you're lying, it will become a problem," Devin explained. "Got a bitch already. This shit is making me tight, G."

Brittany hung up.

At the bar drinking a double of Avion Tequila, Devin was trying to gather his thoughts. *Brittany has me so confused. She is gorgeous though. Five-five, with hazel eyes, black long hair, curvy hips...met her at the mall a few months back,* he thought to himself. *Met the lovely Loyalty a month after. Loyalty was quiet and reserved about her bag. Shit, being from Cleveland was hard. Everybody expects you to look out, but when you're fucked up, nobody is around,* Devin thought. *That is why I paved this wave for myself, and my brothers Reese and Malo. My mom was as good as she could be to me, doing a lot on her own to take care of me. Dad was sent to prison. I was fifteen years old when he was sentenced to twenty-five-to-life for murder. He was shipped out to Mansfield Correctional.*

Devin eventually forgot about his dad's existence, when he got older. The streets were all he knew. The impact his mom and dad left behind was some real gangsta shit. *I control damn near every corner of Cleveland and take pride in the shit,* Devin thought.

Devin finishing his drinks. "Alright call me if y'all need anything," he said, speaking to staff. "Going home to get my mind right. Be back in a few hours," he said, talking to the sexy bartenders.

"OK, no problem. Everything should be fine," the young lady said, making a drink for a customer.

Devin, leaving out, sent Loyalty a quick message. *Baby, I love you and adore everything about you.* He inserted a pickle emoji, and then sent it. Devin went home to his honeycomb in Shaker to rest.

CHAPTER 7:

CREAMER

August 15, 2017

"What's up, Nigga? What you doing?" Devin said, aggressively speaking.

A guy with holes in his clothes said, "Just going to cop something from him," he said, pointing to one of the Creme soldiers, not aware of the Creme power. Approaching the drips...*lick!* Devin smacked the nigga across the face—the guy fell down. Devin lifted his size eleven Airs on his face, stomping him until he was tired.

"This my block, and don't ever come back either speaking bold and honest," he said. Holy-pants dude ran away and did not look back. "Fuck wrong with him, talking to one of my comrades."

The strong, handsome, not regular, irregular type guy jumped in the Tesla Model 3 to count his money. He laughed to himself, "All this money."

Devin called Brittany. "So now you call me? You missed another ultrasound appointment yesterday." Brittany was angry and yelling.

"Man chill out. My bad," Devin told Brittany. "Been busy and need a test done for sure though," Creme said, in confidence.

"Listen, Goofy Ass Nigga, don't play with me. This baby all yours," Brittany was yelling.

Devin explained to Brittany, "My girl is not gone take this shit well. Period. Fucking up everything I got going, Brittany. Now, my first child, you're carrying all of a sudden." He shook his head. "This baby is a surprise to me."

"Man up and do your fucking duties, Baby Daddy."

Devin hung up, quick. He was sitting at the light on Stokes, downtown Euclid. *What am I doing?* Devin thought. Loyalty meant everything to Devin. He pulled the phone off the charger to dial. The phone rang.

"Baby," he said. Devin felt hype to hear Loyalty's voice.

"Hey, glad you called...excuse me," Loyalty said, talking to her staff. "Have to take this call." Loyalty walked into the bathroom at work.

"You working, Love?"

"Yes," Loyalty whispered.

"I love you, Loyalty. You mean so much to me," Devin said, smiling.

"Awe, Babe, I love you, too."

"I need—we need—to talk about something love," Creme said, stuttering.

"Alright, about what?" Loyalty sounded nervous.

"Wanted to take you around to see a couple spots with me, soon as you get off, get dressed," Devin told Loyalty. "Ever since we met, Loyalty, it has been nothing but joy and good times. Thank you for bringing peace into my world, My Love," Devin said, speaking sincerely.

"Same here," Loyalty agreed. "Just don't ever be afraid to talk to me. Off at three-thirty today," Loyalty said, looking at the clock in the bathroom. It read only two-thirty. "Will call you, Baby, when making it home," Loyalty told Devin before hanging up. "I love you." She hung up.

Five p.m. rolled around, and Devin headed over to Loyalty's house to pick her up. Pulling up to the gated community, he sat at the intercom, puzzled. A loud horn blew. In his rear view was a gold G-Wagon, impatient as fuck. Raising his voice, he pushed the damn code in before he beat whomever was behind him the fuck up.

In the driveway, he was thinking hard that telling Loyalty he may have a child on the way would not fix anything. *Just keep it to myself,* he decided, honking the horn. *I'm outside,* he sent a text.

A few moments later, he thought, *there goes my baby,* as he was busting down a shell to roll up before leaving out the driveway. *Baby was fine. She wore a Chanel jumpsuit with a white tee underneath. A boss bitch,* Devin thought. *She has to be, doing paralegal work.*

"Baby, missed you so much," Loyalty said, reaching to give him a hug.

"Missed you, too, Loyalty," he said, backing out the driveway into the sunset with his baby girl. "Here," he said, passing her the blunt.

"Just a drinker, no thanks," she said, while her hand sat on her face.

"Take this, Dude," he said, sounding controlling. Loyalty looked at him, and then took the blunt to inhale. She coughed a few times.

"This is strong," she said, smiling at Devin. He laughed at her.

"That means it worked, Baby," Devin told Loyalty, caressing her chin. "Onto the east side," he said. Devin had a small talk with Loyalty to see where her head was. "You know my nickname?" Devin asked, looking into Loyalty's eyes.

"No, you have not told me, Babe," Loyalty said, looking curious.

"People call me Creme," Devin said. "Listen, don't share this information with everyone," he explained. "One of the biggest drug lords here in Cleveland. Nothing but respect out here for me. Five dope houses, own two bars, and came from literally nothing, Sweetheart, so call me greedy and need it all," Devin explained to Loyalty, rubbing his chin. "A man sacrificing, having to become great, My Love," Devin said, talking to Loyalty. "Do you understand?" he looked at Loyalty's reaction.

"Understand," Loyalty said, sitting in shock. "Why keep this from me, Devin?" Loyalty said, feeling betrayed and lost. "I work for the law," Loyalty stressed to Devin-Creme. Her career meant everything to her. "This is what you tell me now, huh?" Loyalty said, disappointed.

"Baby, don't do this," Creme said, feeling guilty. "Mines is yours and I will support you and kill anybody who feels otherwise about this right now." He pulled up to a huge brick building that seemed so familiar to Loyalty. It looked like the building where she caught her father smoking dope. Loyalty put her head down, ashamed.

"I will be right back," Creme told Loyalty, then rushed out the car into the brick building. As Loyalty sat in the car, her stomach started to hurt, feeling sick for some reason, and ready to leave already. A couple minutes went by and he came out, but with only a black garbage bag. Devin walked to the back of the car, opening the truck, dumping the bag, and quickly getting back inside the car.

"What was that?" Loyalty asked.

"Fifteen hundred dollars," he replied, looking in and out of his rearview mirrors constantly, at the same time grinning and smiling at her while looking away.

Before dropping off Loyalty, he noticed that Loyalty was not saying much. It was a weird vibe between them, which was unusual.

"Well, give you a call later," Loyalty said, looking unsure.

"Alright, Baby, see you soon," he said, waiting for her to enter the house before pulling off and beeping the horn.

Loyalty looks at me differently but, I know she will once shit gets out about the baby, Creme thought to himself. "Damn," he said out loud, punching his car horn.

CHAPTER 8:

SWISHER SWEET

Loyalty, exhausted from going to work, had to make money regardless. All of the staff expected her to come to work in the morning and do an excellent job—that was the impression that Loyalty usually left. She walked in the building, and passed the metal detectors to the elevator, pushing the arrow up moving the elevator pushing twenty upwards.

Twenty minutes later, a young man who was about nineteen years old was before Judge Alex. Judge Alex was an older guy with sandy hair, a pointy nose, and an eager, strict attitude. He continued to ask the young man, "How will you plea?" Judge Alex looked at the boy, ready to send him to jail ASAP.

"Your Honor, plead not guilty," the young guy said, looking directly at Judge Alex in fury. The young boy's nose was flaring; Judge Alex looked over to the young man's lawyer, reading the young boy's charges over. Judge Alex told him to return in two weeks for sentencing. The young man wore an orange jumpsuit with shackles on his feet and hands and headed back to his cell staring deviously. The officers walked the young man back, aggressively.

Loyalty reviewed the cases, writing, and typing up different cases. Hours had passed, and Loyalty was tired and ready to leave. She received a text from Brittany. *Are you busy today? Wanted to invite you to lunch?*

Loyalty responded: *Not today, tired still at work. How is the baby doing?*

Text from Brittany: *The baby is growing fast; appetite is crazy lol.*

Loyalty responded: *That is good for Brittany. Coming to the next appointment.* Loyalty wanted what was best for Brittany. *We need to talk about your child's father. Have you even told Grandma Joy?*

Brittany replied: *Have not. Still a bit nervous of Grandma Joy reaction and all. Call mama now!!* Loyalty texted back to Brittany.

Loyalty acts as if she is better than me, Brittany thought on the way downtown Cleveland to see Creme. Her stomach was full from the nachos and cheese that she ate an hour ago from a local gas station. Brittany was tired of Loyalty always bossing her around—it was bad enough Loyalty made a lot of money. Brittany felt like a peasant.

"Everything Loyalty has will be one day mine," Brittany said to herself with an evil laugh as she was pulling in The Alibi parking lot, eager to see Creme. She loved everything about him. Stepping out of the car and walking across the street to the bar/lounge, she saw that Creme's car was parked directly in front of the door. She put her arms up, and security padded her down for weapons.

Watching Creme talk to one of the strippers made Brittany furious. "What does she want?" Brittany asked, rushing inside and flicking the stripper's hand off Creme's shoulder.

"Chill out, you not my bitch," Creme said, getting in Brittany's face. He was aggravated.

"This is what you were doing here, huh?" Brittany yelled at Creme.

"I make money, Bitch. You know this. What you're here for?" Creme faced Brittany with his arms crossed.

In an honest tone she said, "Anyway, need one thousand dollars," Brittany said, holding her hand out. Creme went into his pockets, pulled out a wop of cash, and then handed Brittany what she asked for.

"Here," Creme said. "See you later, Brittany." Creme pointing at the door.

"No! I will see you later…at the ultrasound appointment," Brittany yelled as she was leaving out The Alibi.

Brittany thought about how Creme made her feel like shit, and she could see that he did not like her. Brittany felt like nothing to him and needed to come up and quickly.

Creme's phone rang. "Hello. Got a drip to hit one hundred-K," Brittany said, smiling through the phone, explaining the lick, then hanging up shortly after.

"I'll call you back." Creme hung up.

* * *

Arriving home from a long day at work, in bed, Loyalty took her shoes off, reached over, and grabbed her phone off of the nightstand to call Devin. The phone rang.

"Baby, how are you?" she asked. Loyalty was glad to hear his voice on the phone.

"Making these moves, My Love," Creme said, sounding tired.

"Be safe, it's a lot going on in Cleveland right now, love you," Loyalty said, concerned.

"I'm good Loyalty. Nobody fucking with me. Got the city on lock," Creme spoke in confidence.

"Well listen, missed a period so will just let a couple days go by to determine anything," Loyalty explained to Creme.

"Abortion is not an option," Creme said.

Loyalty responded, sounding scared. "Wow, damn Baby."

Creme was shocked. "Here for you if you need me, Loyalty."

"Alright, Devin. Keep you posted, Baby. Love you. Bye." Loyalty hung up.

Shit is going crazy, now! Loyalty may be pregnant, too? Creme thought, dropping his head in his lap. Creme was feeling crazy, looking into the thin air while holding the steering wheel. *Loyalty means so much to me,* Creme thought, afraid to lose her due to his secret shadows. He knew it was the game, though.

On the way to Warrensville Heights to see his brothers Reese and Malo, his right-hand men, Creme needed to sit and talk with the guys. Reese and Creme had always been close—they all had each other, right or wrong. Malo had known him since his toddler days, and now Malo was thirty-three and Creme was thirty-five.

I love them niggas for sure, Creme thought as he drove. *Fucked hoes together, hit drips with each other, and sent niggas up top in all for respect.* Pulling up to the Walford apartments, he knew that Malo and Reese had those apartments on lock all over. He buzzed.

"Come up, Brah," Reese told Creme through the intercom. Creme opened the door, and Malo came out with a 9mm Glock that Malo put it in Creme face. Malo and Reese laughed.

"Nigga, stop playing," Creme said, smacking Malo's hand down and walking into the apartment, dapping Reese up.

"Man, this nigga," Reese said, laughing.

"This nigga coming to the door pulling stix out on people like this? Call-a-Duty and shit," Creme said, upset and giving Reese and Malo a goofy look.

"Nigga been on some paranoid shit. You could have been anybody, Nigga," Malo said, holding the gun and looking at Creme. He walked back into the apartment and sat the gun on the table.

Creme spoke while rubbing his hands together. "Anyway, nigga got this drip for us, one hundred bands, you down?" Creme told Malo, confidently.

"Yeah, Nigga," Malo said.

"Hell yeah," Reese agreed, smacking his knee.

"Let's do this," Creme said.

CHAPTER 9:

RECOGNIZE REAL

October fifteenth was Loyalty's birthday, and she was turning twenty-two. It felt good to Loyalty. She was receiving an early bonus from work, and making close to forty thousand dollars a month, which was unreal, but true. She was young, successful, and in love with the most handsome man on the planet. She was also expecting a child, but only two months pregnant.

Loyalty made plans at the Pinstripe to have dinner with Devin and his brothers later in the day. The atmosphere was nice at the Pinstripe. While in the shower, Loyalty lathered her body down with Chanel body gel. Loyalty has not talked to Brittany in about two weeks. Brittany had been pushing Loyalty to the side, and communication had just been distant.

Brittany didn't even know Loyalty was pregnant, although Loyalty did tell Grandma Joy, though she had her promise not to tell Brittany anything. Loyalty didn't want Brittany to know she was pregnant. As for Brittany's job: Loyalty fired her months ago, so Brittany held resentment towards Loyalty. Both sisters were pregnant and didn't even talk as much. Loyalty also still hadn't met the father of Brittany's baby yet, which was weird. Loyalty decided to mind her business.

Drying off, Loyalty applied Shea coconut oil on her body, grabbing the dress off the bed that Creme had bought. A Chanel dress, and shoes, with a seven-carat diamond bracelet.

She parked outside Pinstripe early, at six p.m. and Loyalty called Creme to meet her outside.

The phone rang. "Sup, Baby?" Creme answered. "Where are you?"

"I am outside," Loyalty said, yelling a little at Creme being funny.

"Man, watch your mouth, coming now," Creme told Loyalty, and they both hung up. Loyalty locked the car and walking towards the door. Creme met Loyalty, smiling, and holding hands, and they walked into Pinstripe where people were laughing, drinking, and doing some business. "You look beautiful," Creme said, looking Loyalty up and down to compliment her.

"Thanks, Baby," Loyalty said, blushing at Creme words, and walking up the stairs towards the outside patio. "Let's grab a drink first."

"How can I help you?" the bartender, a five-foot-sight young woman with deep dimples asked while wiping off some clean glasses.

"Yes, a double of patron with lime. Babe, what are you having?" she looked at Creme for his response.

"Double of Hennessey," he said. They grabbed their drinks, headed towards the balcony, and met up with crème's bros. The wood fire was burning, and the sky was getting dim. Both Reese and Malo got up to approach them. "What's up, Bra?" crème's spoke proudly to each of the men. "This is my wife, my baby Loyalty." They all gave hugs and sat around the bonfire.

"How are you? My name is Terrance, but everyone calls me Reese though Beautiful," Reese introduced himself to Loyalty, giving the lover boy vibe. "Damn," he said, looking at Loyalty from head to toe.

"My name is Malo, Baby Girl. Creme is my right hand. Did you know that?"

"Had no idea," Loyalty replied.

"So, how old are you?" Reese asked Loyalty. Creme was looking done with the games already.

"Chill out, Niggas. Be cool. Y'all buggin for real. This my baby fix that questioning shit," Creme told them in a serious tone.

"Yeah, yeah," Reese said what he meant. "OK everyone chill out and relax." Malo sat there quiet. He knew Creme was not to be fucked with for real. He said what he meant. Afterwards, they all took a sip out of their crystal glasses.

"Nice to meet you both, and thank y'all for coming out tonight," Loyalty said. She sat there wondering why no one had asked about her pregnancy yet, and wondered if they even knew?

"Excuse me, Guys," Loyalty said. She had to go to the bathroom. Loyalty walked to the bathroom, and her head started to pound. She felt dizzy and sick. *I keep drinking. Creme asked me to stop, and I completely ignored him every time,* she thought to herself as she wiped her face and sat her head and back against the wall. Looking for her phone in her purse, she scrolled for Chanel's number. Loyalty decided to call Chanel for some type of energy, advice, or anything to make her feel better.

The phone rang. "Hey, Babe, what's up?" Chanel answered the phone in a joyful tone.

"Hey, Chanel there is so much we have to talk about. Can I come over later?" Loyalty asked Chanel. Yes, you may, Loyalty. Anytime. When you get ready, I will be here."

"OK!" Loyalty spoke into the phone, sounding a little better. "Talk to you in a few."

Loyalty washed her hands from the throw up, looked in the mirror, and then exited out back towards the balcony.

"You OK?" Creme asked, concerned.

"Yes, I'm fine, Baby," she said, and sat down to endure in the conversation.

An hour passed, until Creme looked at both Malo and Reese. Loyalty grabbed her feet while Creme said, "Let's go. I love you, Loyalty," Creme explained to her, while headed towards her car.

"I love you, too, Devin. Thank you for everything, Handsome Man," Loyalty said, smiling at Creme as they waited for the valet. Creme was kissing all over Loyalty and making her feel amazing and loved. "I will call you later, Baby," Loyalty said, smiling at Creme.

"Make sure you do, Loyalty. Don't want to come looking for you," Crème said laughing, but serious about his response.

Loyalty sat in her car, thinking how Brittany had become so distant. Loyalty just needed Chanel for her support in that moment. Loyalty, on the way to Chanel's house, stopped at a nearby gas station in Maple Heights for bottled water.

The cashier said, "Hi, is this all for you?"

"Yes, sir," Loyalty responded by pulling money from her Gucci purse.

"Your total is one-ten."

Loyalty sat in the car for a moment before pulling off. Chanel stayed by herself in a two-bedroom on a street called Sunny Slope Drive. No children, and both her parents stayed in Cleveland Heights with their dog named Grace, no sisters, and four brothers. Chanel had been Loyalty's best friend since freshman year in college. They met when she couldn't get her candy out the machine for some reason and then decided to push onto the machine while the candy fell. "Girl, you don't have to," she said, and Chanel looking pleased.

"It was nothing, Girl, these things are always giving me a hard time," she said. They both laughed. "Well maybe sometimes."

"Well maybe sometime if you are free, we could link up or something after our classes?"

"Cool, no problem."

Chanel handed her a piece of paper with her number on it. Chanel was five-two, brown skinned, with hazel eyes, and a very athletic body. She was very girly, but just a dear friend. She was very honest and loyal. A year ago, she lost her baby in her cousin's bathroom on the floor, only at twelve weeks. Chanel was depressed and was numb to life—blaming herself, crying etc. It was not her fault. Chanel had been eating and drinking healthy lately, and both confused on the loss. She was nervous and stressed about telling her parents because she was not married.

Loyalty knocked on the door. Chanel opened the door with open arms. "Hey, Babe," Chanel said, smiling.

She was wearing a red Adidas jumpsuit and socks to match. *Super dope,* Loyalty thought. "Hey, Bitch," Loyalty said, smiling.

"Come in," Chanel told Loyalty. Chanel hugged Loyalty, after she took off her shoes at the door. "Finally! Loyalty at the kitchen table; girl you gasping for air like you were running from the police!" They laughed, although Chanel was kind of serious about her question. "Some eggs and bacon?" Chanel asked.

"Yes, love some," Loyalty said, sitting at the table ready to eat. Chanel was very excited to see Loyalty.

"I have a surprise for you," Loyalty said, standing up from the wooden chair to reveal her pregnant belly. Chanel was surprised. Loyalty said, "I'M PREGNANT!"

Chanel lost her shit and screamed. "Awwwww!" Chanel hugged on Loyalty and explained to Loyalty. "You need help with my God baby, let me know." Loyalty explained that Devin had been a little distant lately. "Loyalty don't be worried; Cream works all the time. He loves you," she said, trying to cheer Loyalty's spirits up. "Loyalty, why you tripping, Sis?"

CHAPTER 10:

LOVE ME NOT

Loyalty went into work in the morning feeling a little better than her usual few mornings of sicknesses. Loyalty enjoyed her birthday and spent the day with Creme and Chanel. Loyalty entered the building, and everyone greeted her. Loyalty loved the fact that respect came instantly from her line of work.

"Hey, Sam, did you finish the Peterson paperwork?"

"Sure, all finished and it's ready to go." Sam handed over the paperwork to Loyalty for review. "Good luck," Sam said.

Loyalty walked into the office and already had six missed calls. Lunch was in two hours, and Loyalty decided to go over some missed calls. The phone began ringing. Looking at the ID, she saw that it was that damn Brittany.

"Hey Sis, the baby is due next month—am excited. Sorry for missing your appointments. Been very busy, Britt, plus you never really call," Loyalty said, annoyed.

"It's cool," Brittany responded, flicking with her fingernails. "Well, coming over tomorrow. Want to do some catching up?"

Loyalty was sitting at her desk as thoughts kept running throughout her head. *I knew now that I didn't want Brittany to visit*, she thought.

"Sure Britt," Loyalty said, seeming unsure of her answer. "Off at six p.m. tomorrow. Don't be late!"

"Cool. See you then."

Loyalty took a sip of V8 Splash, she began looking through emails, wrote a few notes for court, and prepared some files to copy. While on her Apple laptop, she went to the search engine and typed in "Devin Rose" on the database. Her eyes widened: so much came up! Two warrants for obstruction, manslaughter, and assault.

I cannot believe what is in front of me, Loyalty thought. *The shit almost made no sense at all.* She quickly got off the page and sat in her chair, puzzled and confused all at once. Loyalty picked up her head and continued to work instead of pondering on something she could not change.

* * *

Thinking of Loyalty all day, Devin was sick in bed. *No outside for me right now,* he thought as the phone rang. "Hello?" Devin answered in a happy tone.

"How are you? I have not heard from you in a while, Devin," Loyalty said, sounding pissed.

"Calm down, Baby. I have been in bed all day sick as a dog. How have you been, Sweetheart?"

"I'm just not getting it," she said, furious. "It is going on twelve noon. You do remember we have an appointment Friday, Mister, so don't forget." Loyalty had been super moody lately, and distant.

I really don't know what is up with her; I will see though, Devin thought to himself. He looked through his phone to call Brittany. The phone rang.

"Sup, Girl."

"Hey, Cream. Can I help you today? Would you like some good pussy, or nah?" she said, sounding devious.

Creme laughed. "I'm good. Come over. We need to talk about that drip you was talking about. ASAP."

"OK, on my way now."

Brittany is mad annoying, but on the other hand is down for whatever, whenever, Devin thought to himself. *I loved that shit. Now she is carrying my baby, met Brittny at Alibi about a year ago. Brittany was lit on the pole, plus baby was gorgeous. Pretty big face, brown eyes, short, and also interesting.*

Devin sat up in bed, rubbing his head and then got up to undress, He headed to the shower; the water was his therapy. Walking naked to the shower, Devin kept thinking of Loyalty and what telling her the truth would do to their relationship. For the first time in a long time, he was scared, and ashamed of his actions. Creme shook his head in the water, then put his head down as the water fell down his body.

* * *

Walking into Creme house, Brittany seductively had Gucci pumps on with a trench coat with nothing under. His door was already open for her. Creme's house was already big, and nice for a man that lives here.

Stepping into the shower, everything was exactly the way she planned it to be. "Hey, Daddy," Brittany said, kissing his chest while caressing his dick.

"Turn around, Brittany," Creme said, grabbing her ponytail—she was doing whatever he asked. He began to rub his dick up and down her ass then slowly pushed it in. Moaning over and over from the extreme pleasures, Creme slapped her ass while she was throwing it back for his dick to catch.

"Let's get in the bed. We need to talk," Creme said, feeling relieved. Brittany followed him behind.

"Your belly is big as hell, Bra," Creme said, laughing.

"OK, so what? Anyway, this girl has at least one-hundred thousand in her account," Brittany spoke, using her hands.

"Is that right?" Creme said, rubbing his chest hair. "Where the chick stay?"

"Well, I am the brain, and you be the muscle. She stays on the west side."

"Cool, just let me know when and where. I gotta pee. I will be right back," Devin said. As he walked to the bathroom, Brittany sat up to stare at him while lying in his Versace sheets in a daze.

Oh, I just love his fine ass, she thought to herself. Still covered with the sheets, Brittany walked over to the dresser to pick up his phone. *I can't believe my fucking eyes: my sister had been calling this nigga!*

Brittany went through their messages, and then dropped the phone. "This bitch is pregnant? What the hell?"

"What the fuck are you doing, Bitch?" Creme asked.

Brittany kept yelling. "You got my sister pregnant? You got my sister pregnant?" she screamed, looking raged at Creme Alsadi. "My sister your wife, huh?" she asked, staring into his eyes.

"Yeah, Brittany, that's my girl. I didn't know she even had a sister. Never brought you up once."

"I bet! Fuck that dork-ass bitch," Brittany said, rolling her eyes.

"Listen, watch your mouth," Creme added.

"Man, fuck that. Does she know I'm pregnant? The baby is yours. If not, she will find out if you don't do what I ask you to do," Brittany said. Creme was getting angry, but not showing her. "Set her up she got one-hundred thousand dollars in her account." Brittany stood looking at him like a villain. He nodded his head yes.

"Could you please leave? I have to get my shit together," he said. Brittany laughed.

"Sure. See you next week at six a.m. I have a plan. Understood, Baby?" she said, rubbing his face.

"Yeah, whatever man," he said, waving her off.

She blew a kiss at Crème. *Nobody cared about me, so why should I care?* Brittany thought with a grin across her face as she exited.

As soon as Brittany left, Devin broke down into tears smacking his head, frustrated at his actions. *Can't take anything back right now. I have to follow through with the plans. Get this over with so Brittany can be on her way. Of course, I am ashamed and scared of Loyalty finding about my secret shadows that follow me.*

Creme picked up the phone to go over a few things with Reese and Malo like always. They agreed; he told them to be careful because Loyalty was pregnant, and to never mention Brittany's grimy ass.

CHAPTER 11:

TROPICAL BLEND

Leaving from the Justice Center, it had been a very long and busy day. Loyalty had so much work lined up for her for the next day. Driving on the freeway, it was about an eight-to-ten-minute drive home with many lights, on such a bright beautiful day out. The sun was shining very eloquently.

Loyalty punched in the gate code. Approaching the driveway, Loyalty noticed a purple vase with white lilies on the front porch. Loyalty looked outside of the vehicle, looking to see if anyone was close or walking away from the house. With no one around, Loyalty noticed the streets were pretty clear; no kids out. No nothing. Loyalty began to feel paranoid for some odd reason.

Loyalty thought the flowers could be from Devin. Walking near the steps and locking the car door, she saw that the vase had a black note hanging on the side of it with a black balloon string. Loyalty picked up the letter to read: *Your deepest darkest Secrets are now my Secrets.* Loyalty dropped the note, leaving the flowers, and entering the inside of the house. Loyalty began panicking, turning on the alarm, and then closing the door.

Loyalty, taking off her shoes—Steve Madden shoes—looking inside her purse for the phone, she tried calling Devin several times, but the phone was just ringing. It went to voicemail. Loyalty shook her head, feeling upset that Creme just didn't care. For two days, Loyalty had been trying to call and text Devin with no answer. Loyalty redialed Devin's number again and rubbed her stomach, experiencing sharp pains.

The phone rang.

"Hey, Love," Creme said in a tired tone.

"Really? Two days, Devin!" Loyalty said, pissed at Creme. "No calls, huh? Weird shit. Talk to me." Loyalty said with her hands on her hips, walking back and forth, rapidly pacing.

"Baby, been busy lately. Loyalty, I apologize, Beautiful," Creme said, sounding sincere.

"This is bogus. I'm pregnant," Loyalty said, talking into the phone at Creme. "You know what Creme—Devin, whatever your name is—fuck you."

"Loy...." Creme uttered, but Loyalty hung up on him quickly.

He tried dialing Loyalty back-to-back, but there was no answer. Creme felt a bit numb. Devin closed the flip phone to continue driving across Martin Luther King to drop off some shit to his drip. Creme decided to distance away from Loyalty altogether. In two more days, Creme had planned on going into Loyalty's house to grab her. He shook his head, feeling like a straight slime. Part of Creme cared, and a part of him didn't. *All to keep Brittany baby secret,* he thought to himself.

The phone rang. It was Reese calling.

"What's up, Bra?" Creme answered with deep base in his voice.

"You got the info?" Reese sounded impatient.

"Yeah, Nigga. Shit go be quick like a rabble," Creme said, looking out the rear mirror.

"Not trying to send her up, but shit...one hundred babies sound good right now," Reese said, smiling through the phone.

"Nigga, that's my BM," Creme said, turning, telling Reese forcefully. Creme turned the radio down.

"Yeah, but you still boxing her in regardless, though. Anyway, Nigga, just hit me up later," Reese told Creme before hanging up.

* * *

Around seven that night, while sitting in the living room at the end of the round table counting up at least eighty thousand—smiling—Creme was there for two hours counting his money.

"Can have any bitch," Creme said, laughing, as he stroked his own ego. Money felt like pleasure to Creme: he was addicted, foolish, greedy, and refused to slow down. Even if it meant crossing someone who was close to him. If anyone thought he had it all, he didn't feel he did. Love came last; cash came fast.

The phone rang. It was Loyalty calling. Loyalty was laughing. "We don't know what we are having yet until the baby is born."

"That's cool, we have a man child."

"Ready for that?" Loyalty asked.

Creme put down his money to twist his dread, and seductively speak to Loyalty. "I'm always ready," Creme said, surprised he was turned on. "Take off your clothes," he said, hanging up. He needed her body, smell, and laugh, he thought to himself.

* * *

Brittany was sitting outside Creme's house parked in a Charger 2016 rental with black tint—she had been following Creme for two days to see if he would go over to Loyalty's house. No luck. Turning the key to the dark tint in the Charger after seeing someone look out of the window, she sped up the street passing the two stop signs away from his house.

Creme looked out of his living room window and saw a blue Charger with dark tint. *Nobody knew where I stayed except Loyalty and Brittany, Reese, and Malo. It was that hoe Brittany—had to be. This chick was watching my house,* Creme thought to himself, annoyed. *Brittany gone get hers back tenfold, baby mama or not. She deserves it,* Creme thought, putting on his Gucci hoodie.

Creme walked out to his car thinking to himself. *We can play this game, just to keep your mouth shut then. Brittany also carried my first child...ole rat ass was due any moment now.*

Pulling up to the gate at Loyalty's house, he typed in the gate code and drove in quietly to see his girl. In the driveway, Creme started feeling guilty about everything that was going on behind Loyalty's back. Loyalty was now five months pregnant with Creme's second child and here he was putting them both in danger.

He got out of the Tesla a bit anxious, looking to make sure he was not being followed there. Creme rushed up to the door to knock.

"Hey," he said. Loyalty was everything Creme could ever want. He leaned in to kiss her forehead.

"Devin, come in," Loyalty said, sounding peaceful. She was dressed in a sexy skintight Fashion Nova dress, with her hair curly. She was everything Devin could ever want.

"Loyalty, I thought I told you to be naked," Creme said, smiling at Loyalty.

She slowly slid her dress down. Underneath it was her bare ass and knee-high socks. As the dress fell to the floor, she crawled over to him as he sat on the couch and started to unzip his pants while looking him in his eyes.

"Suck this dick with all your heart, you hear me?" Creme said, licking his lips. Loyalty slid her mouth down his dick, warm and full of it as he pushed her head up and down, fast...slow...his dick grew bigger and harder. Loyalty gagged. Creme laughed, keeping Loyalty's head up and down at a pace he wanted.

Picking up Loyalty, he moved to the kitchen, moving her paperwork and seasoned jars out of the way, scooting her ass onto the counter. He opened her legs wide, and Creme gripped her tits, sliding all of his dick in her, kissing Loyalty's forehead over and over. Loyalty's pussy was warm and throbbing.

"Turn around," Creme demanded of Loyalty. Loyalty smacked her ass, and Creme gripped Loyalty hips. Everything about her turned Creme on— even the moans.

CHAPTER 12:

NARCISSIST

Creme woke up, looking into the phone. The time read four-thirty a.m. He hopped out the bed with Loyalty to use the bathroom, washed his face, and then stood to see the reflection in the mirror to see the man who he had become. He exited the bathroom to watch Loyalty sleep.

So peacefully, Creme thought, as he stood over the bed. He grabbed and put on his shoes and clothes, quietly to leave, kissed Loyalty's forehead, then left without a trace. Creme was on the way to Alibi to check on things before going home. While leaving Loyalty's driveway, the phone rang. Creme looked at the phone and saw it was a drip calling. He forwarded it to voicemail, then proceeded to the freeway.

The phone rang. "Reese, wasup?" Creme was inpatient.

Reese the wiped the cold out his eyes before speaking. "Sup, Nigga?"

"Call Bean. Why that nigga still calling me?" Creme hung up shortly after. Bean was a young dude from 131st. *Funny, he went to college and spent a lot of money,* Creme thought. *Over three thousand a month. Easy money. Big spenders get an answer, other than that...business need to be run.*

The phone rang. "What the fuck, Man?" Creme said as he picked up, annoyed.

Brittany said, "Baby on the way to your house," while twirling her hair.

"Chill out with all that *baby* shit. Be on the way once I'm finished doing what am doing," Creme explained aggressively.

"Creme, we was just fucking, now I can't call you baby?" Brittany was confused but pressed.

"Don't give a fuck, Bitch, see you later," Creme banged on Brittany.

Creme made Brittany sick, she thought, still looking at the phone. Shocked. Brittany felt obsessed with Creme; no matter what, she desired him more each day. No matter what, Brittany needed to have him around. No matter the cost. Brittany was on her way to see Creme at his house...to wait for him. Brittany wanted to go over the plan about how to destroy her sister Loyalty. Brittany sat quietly in Creme's driveway, eating her fruit bowl.

An hour passed, and Creme pulled up blasting Kevin Gates. Brittany got out immediately to meet him.

"Wasup, Baby Mama?" Creme rushed past Brittany to get to the front door. Brittany took a seat at a Creme round marble black table, and explained she was ready to begin her demise.

"So, here is the plan. Have a gold Caravan to drive there," she said.

Creme replied. "Reese, Malo will be there to make sure everything is cool."

Creme began counting the money that he collected from the bar at the night club.

"Cool, you and the guys chill in the car while I distract her," Brittany expressed with no remorse. "After that...bam! You guys come rushing in to take Loyalty to this abandoned warehouse downtown Cleveland, until she gives up everything," Brittany said, feeling unregretful. Creme stopped counting his money to look at Brittany in disgust. "Ten p.m. Monday night," Brittany explained, then started to focus on why Creme's phones kept ringing.

Brittany walked over to Creme seductively. Creme uttered, "Nah, we good Brittany." Creme pushed Brittany out of his space. Brittany didn't give up so easily; Britany attempted to move closer to cream once more. Creme pushed Brittany even harder out his face. Brittany frowned, with her face in anger.

"Brittany you not my girl," Creme told her aggressively, pocking Brittany in the head with his finger. Creme had no remorse for his feelings for Brittany. "Let's hit this drip, then I am taking care of the kid. That's that, Fam," Creme said, yelling, and using his hands while looking in Brittany's eyes.

"Be with me, Creme. I love you," Brittany said, begging Creme. He became instantly pissed, moving into the kitchen for space to think.

"Yeah, that's why you setting up your only sister," Creme said, sternly.

"Fuck you! Nigga," Brittany yelled, upset. Brittany grabbed her purse and then headed for the door.

"Bitch!" Creme said, as the door shut, and tears fell from Brittany's face. *Fuck that dog ass hoe, Brittany. Don't understand why this is even happening— maybe it's my greed,* he thought.

Brittany thought to herself, *Loyalty brainwashing Creme, she is done. Let's get this party started.* Brittany drove off from Creme driveway with an evil grin, picking up her phone. It rang.

"Hello," Loyalty spoke loudly.

"Hey, Sis, what are you doing?" Brittany asked anxious, and ungenuine.

"What do you think? I do have a job, Brittany. It's five in the morning," Loyalty explained, feeling confused and annoyed.

"OK, going to stop over later, if that's OK with you?" Brittany asked.

"Sure, cooking later...you can join me," Loyalty told Brittany, surprised, as she put on her work clothes.

"Sounds great," Brittany said, rolling her eyes.

"Brittany, you been OK?" Loyalty asked, out of concern for her sister.

"Good. This baby growing on me," Brittany explained, rubbing her belly as she sat on the coffee-colored sofa. "How have you been, Loyalty? Been hiding lately... you not pregnant too, are you?" Brittany asked while covering her mouth, snickering jokingly.

Loyalty removed the phone off her ear before replying, "Girl, me and man not having babies right now," Loyalty responded, feeling nervous and outed.

Brittany rolled her eyes. "Okay, just saying. See ya later on for dinner," Brittany told Loyalty before hanging up the call.

* * *

Loyalty arrived at work; the staff loved and appreciated Loyalty at work. Walking in the office, she set her laptop on the desk to work on some cases and read some unread messages in her email. Loyalty looked over at the phone and saw that there were several voice messages unheard. She listened to the first message which was a few seconds of silence, then...*Bang Bang*...gun shots! The person who recorded the foolish behavior hung up. Loyalty shook her head and sat in a daze before deleting the voicemail.

Anxious and, confused Loyalty thought, *First the letter, now this*. She picked up her MK bag off the floor to make a call on her cell, still shaking up from the voicemail.

The phone rang. "Hey, Girl," Chanel picked up sounding bubbly.

"Girl, at work listening to this voicemail. Somebody doing some major stalking, sending me notes, and then gunshots to my work voicemail." Loyalty was pissed, holding her hand to her head.

"Loyalty, you have to tell someone at the job. Seriously, this is getting out of hand," Chanel said, pacing her living room, afraid for her friend.

"I don't understand what to do, or even what is going on," Loyalty explained to Chanel while shaking her head. She then got up to look at the view from her office.

"Love you so much, Loyalty," Chanel told Loyalty while sitting back down slowly on the couch to relax her emotions.

"Ok, love ya! Call you later. Going to give Grandma Joy a call," Loyalty explained before ending the call.

Grandma Joy picked up her phone. "Hello, Baby," Grandma sounded very excited to hear from Loyalty.

"Hey, Mama, how have you been feeling? Been a minute," Loyalty explained, feeling guilty.

"Haven't been doing so well, but Mama will be fine. God got me, Baby," Grandma said, proudly speaking. "Was been going on? Haven't heard from you either," Grandma Joy was slurring her words a bit...slowly.

"Have been busy working; tomorrow will be there after work," Loyalty explained, still sitting at the window.

"Okay, Baby. See you tomorrow. Also forgot to ask, how the baby?" Grandma Joy, concerned, asked her.

Loyalty blushed. "Grandma Joy, the baby is good. Growing fast. So excited."

"That's a blessing, Baby. Your sister is about to bust any day now take care of Brittany," Grandma was giggling, and explained to Loyalty before the call ended.

Loyalty looked out the window trying to wrap her head around all the extra drama that had now entered her life—*or had it always been there all along,* she wondered.

CHAPTER 13:

NO DOUBT

Just as she got home from long day at work, her phone rang.

"Hey, Loyalty," Brittany said, sounding excited falsely. "Dinner on for tonight still?" Brittany asked, curiously.

"Yep we are. Have to talk to you about a few things anyway," Loyalty explained, sitting in bed with all her work clothes on, flicking through channels.

"About what?" Brittany asks in suspicion.

"Let you know when you get here," Loyalty said, and soon after ended the call with Brittany. She was watching TV and rubbing her belly. Loyalty looked down to her belly and said, "You will bring me all the joy and happiness," talking to her unborn child. She fell asleep shortly after.

***

Loyalty woke up to the phone ringing. Chanel kept calling. She avoided Chanel's phone call, and then walked over to the master bathroom, flushed the toilet, and then washed her hands. She walking into the kitchen to start cooking; the time was around eight p.m. Loyalty's nap was much needed.

She reached in the fridge and got some vegetables, turkey, and rice. Loyalty prepared the dinner table, placed some gold silverware, and filled the Nautica wine glasses with orange juice. It started to smell so amazing in the kitchen. Loyalty raised her head and closed her eyes to take in the delicious smell, finally taking a short break.

Loyalty noticed that Chanel kept calling, but Loyalty was just too irritated to be bothered. She walked back in the bedroom, put the phone on charge, and then silent to finish dinner.

It was ten p.m. when Loyalty looked at her wall clock. *Brittany should be on her way now it was already late*, she thought. She checked the oven to see if the turkey had finished, and then turned down the heat.

Knock knock.

Loyalty was excited to see her sister. "Coming, Britt," Loyalty yelled while checking the food. Loyalty opened the door to see Brittany standing in front of her, wearing all black, and aiming a 9mm in her face.

"Bitch get in the house," Brittany told her while shoving her with the gun, close to Loyalty's belly. "On the floor," Brittany told Loyalty forcefully. Loyalty did as she was told, quietly lying face down on her living room floor.

"What are you doing, Brittany?" Loyalty asked in shock.

"Hoe, you stole my dude and walk around like you perfect," Brittany explained, putting the gun on Loyalty's forehead. Brittany's phone began to ring. "Wasup!" Brittany answered, out of breath. "Shut up, come in," Brittany said to the person on the other end of the phone.

Laying on the floor, feeling so anxious and angry, Loyalty wondered who Brittany just invited in the house. *Now shit really crazy as f*, she thought.

Brittany walked over to cut the stove off, as the food began to burn.

"Where is the tape?" Brittany spoke to herself, looking through the drawers. Brittany found the tape sitting next to the mail and hurried to duct tape Loyalty before the boys came inside to grab Loyalty.

Creme was speed walking towards Loyalty's house door, leaving the van parked in the driveway, wearing an all-black Nike jumpsuit and black Timberlands. His heart started to beat so fast. *Maybe after all this, Loyalty will forgive me,* he thought. Creme was in for a rude awakening.

Reese and Malo followed behind Creme. Loyalty was there with her eyes and mouth covered shut, crying quietly.

"Man, let's go," Creme told Brittany, while signaling the guys to carry Loyalty out the door. Brittany had been cursing Loyalty out for fun, getting a real kick out of it.

"Nigga be quiet. You the one talking instead of helping lift this bitch up," Brittany replied, feeling lame. Creme waved his hands, rushing them all, including her. Creme, Reese, and Malo picked up Loyalty, lifting her up face down, slowly out the house into the Caravan. Creme was sweating, looking at Loyalty, and feeling so bad that he was so fucked up. His mind was running: *greed would make me do anything, even sacrifice one of my children to live comfortable—not happy—comfortable. I loved Loyalty...or didn't I?*

Creme decided to adjust Loyalty's seat in the back row of the van to lay her down. Brittany closed the house door, rushing out with a smile at the success of kidnapping her only sister.

"Okay, the way to the warehouse won't be long," Brittany told everyone while speeding out the driveway, headed towards the freeway. Brittany looked over at Creme as he stared out the window. *His face is spaced out, as if he is zoned out or something,* Brittany thought. Finally approaching the parking lot, Brittany was determined to find a secure spot. The location was in the flats where it could lead into the warehouse; finally, the car was tucked and secure. Moments later, they all got out the car, rushing and ready to get to business.

* * *

The car stopped, and Loyalty thought over and over about wishing that she answered Chanel's call. Sweat dripped from her face, and her body was sore. Loyalty thought to herself, *I never really realized how bad my relationship with Britany was headed.*

Creme watched as Loyalty was being picked up from the backseat of the van into the warehouse. *Plus, she was pregnant,* Creme thought.

Brittany also watched. *Creme was my everything, not Loyalty,* she thought to herself. *Anything to get Loyalty out the picture, I am all game.* Brittany started to think of what Grandma Joy would say and followed the men into the warehouse with no care in anyone's world. Brittany didn't care if her and Loyalty never talked again, as long as Brittany got what she wanted so desperately: Creme.

Loyalty was forced to sit in a medal cold chair and was sitting in disbelief. Loyalty sat quietly with her head down, thinking and thinking. Betrayed by Brittany, her only sister. It frightened Loyalty.

Malo grabbed Loyalty's face. "Where is the money, Bitch?" he demanded.

Brittany stood watching in disgust, practically enjoying watching Loyalty lose at all costs. They all watched as Loyalty sat there in the same position, not saying a word. Malo tried to reach over and grab Loyalty again. Loyalty somehow felt it was coming, kicking Malo directly in the mouth as hard as she could.

Everyone laughed, except Brittany. Loyalty was angry, in severe shock. Brittany pointed the gun directly at Loyalty, sitting nonchalant.

"Ready to lose everything?" Brittany asked Loyalty, waiting for Loyalty to say anything disrespectful out her mouth. The gun was still pointed, and Brittany held on firmly.

Malo didn't believe what he saw. *The two was sisters, yet both so different,* he thought. Loyalty was well-mannered and reserved. Brittany was loud, and very different with the shits for real.

Loyalty slowly lifted her head. "Fuck your whole life, Stupid Bitch," Loyalty expressed in the calmest way. Brittany smacked Loyalty directly in her face laughing after.

"We'll see," Brittany told Loyalty.

* * *

Chanel was calling Loyalty's phone all night, and it worried the hell out of Chanel. She thought maybe Loyalty was tired. Chanel finally laid back in bed with Loyalty on her mind, watching the phone until she fell asleep.

* * *

Loyalty thought to herself. *The reality is some guys and Brittany are holding me for ransom.* Loyalty started to feel the urge to kill Brittany's ungrateful ass. Loyalty continued to wiggle around in the cold medal chair, starving, and feeling she would snap any moment, Loyalty fell asleep shortly after.

* * *

Creme watched Loyalty till she fell asleep, and until Brittany interrupted him. "Back to business, Lover Boy," Brittany shoved Creme shoulder. "Soon the signatures will be signed, and the money will be ours, Baby," Brittany whispered to Creme, rubbing his dick with the gun.

"Just hurry up," Creme told Brittany, zipping his jacket.

"Where are you going, Daddy?" Brittany asked Cream.

"Bitch, this shit don't stop. Still have business to run," Creme told her, headed towards the door, talking quietly.

Loyalty, pretending to be asleep the whole time, was overhearing Brittany with another familiar voice. Hours passed, and someone came back and talked to Brittany. Listening closely, Loyalty just kept her head down. Someone had approached Loyalty now in force, aimed at her face, causing blood to drip down Loyalty's nose.

"Sign the papers, Bitch," Brittany shoved the papers at Loyalty.

Brittany thinks if I sign the papers, that gives her access to all of my accounts, including savings, technically giving Brittany rights to everything, Loyalty thought.

"Sign the papers or die. Choose one," Brittany explained, walking around Loyalty's chair. Brittany was inpatient, cocky with brass knuckles she used to attack Loyalty.

Creme walked into the warehouse only to see Brittany punching Loyalty around with brass knuckles. "What the fuck?" Creme yelled, slamming and choking Brittany on the dusty wall. Creme was heated.

Loyalty lifted her head in shock, and one tear fell down Loyalty's cheek. *Brittany and Creme were plotting to kill me, at the same time trying to protect me? Bullshit!* Loyalty thought. So many questions passed Loyalty's mind. *How do you guys even know another?* Loyalty thought Creme loved her, and their unborn child.

Brittany walked back towards Loyalty yelling. "Keep talking. Want me to kill her now?" Brittany pointed the gun at Loyalty's head. Creme rushed over, smacking Brittany hard enough to drop the gun.

* * *

Three days after being abducted by Brittany, Loyalty thought about her use-to-be lover, Creme. He had everyone fooled, including Loyalty. Loyalty sat in the cold ass chair feeling restless, hungry.

"Feed me!" Loyalty yelled.

"Shut up, Bitch. You not eating nothing," Brittany replied, smirking.

"Listen, Brittany, leaving out again, this time have to take Reese and Malo with me real quick. Making two stops," Creme told Brittany, looking into her eyes with his hand on her shoulder. "Don't do no dumb shit," Creme told her, reaching for the door.

"OK, what time you be back?" Brittany asked Cream with her hand on one hip, holding the 9mm with a cold expression upon her face.

"Soon," Creme reassured Brittany before leaving out. Creme and Brittany stared at each other. Creme signaled the men and left.

Loyalty will never forgive me for betraying her like this, Creme's thoughts rushed through his head as he was grabbing for the car handle. *Brittany is nine months pregnant carrying my child, can't believe it.*

CHAPTER 14:

REMORSE, REGRET, REPENT

"It's me and you now," Brittany told Loyalty, punching Loyalty in the face and hoping she died already. The greed and anger came from envy Brittany had built over the years.

"Why are you doing this?" Loyalty asked Brittany. Loyalty cried.

"Sign the papers and all of this will be over," Brittany told Loyalty, shoving the papers at Loyalty. Brittany repeated her question and Loyalty began to sit in silence; Loyalty was hurt deeply and wanted revenge. "Well, going to the bathroom, when I return you should be ready to put your raggedy ass signature on the dotted line," Brittany told Loyalty, switching her ass to the bathroom while laughing.

Loyalty started to think quick before Brittany returned. Loyalty started moving through the tape, realizing the diamond bracelet might help. Constantly cutting and cutting through the tape with the bracelet on Loyalty's wrist, it finally came off. She pulled the tape from her eyes with her heart pounding harder by the second. Loyalty put her hand on her chest to calm her down.

* * *

Chanel was worried. Days had passed, and still nothing from Loyalty. Grandma Joy and Chanel made a missing person report. Chanel tried calling Brittany but there was no answer. She was feeling sick and angry. *My best friend is not around to be found. Loyalty was my friend's sister, and I would do anything for her,* Chanel thought as she called Loyalty phone again.

"Hey, you reached Alsadi Monroe, leave a detailed message. Thanks," Loyalty's greeting said.

"I love you," Chanel spoke into the phone, crying, and then shortly hanging up.

* * *

Loyalty looked over at the table next her and saw that little Ms. Brittany had left the 9mm. Loyalty sprinted over quietly to grab the gun, then looked for the bathroom and waited for Brittany to come out.

* * *

Brittany was standing in the mirror, fixing her hair. *Can't wait to take all her money and kill that bastard baby,* she thought while opening the door. *Something doesn't feel right,* Brittany thought. Alsadi came out of nowhere, smacking her with the pistol quickly. Brittany was on the floor holding her face in fear.

"Stupid bitch!" Brittany told Loyalty.

Loyalty shot Brittany in the face twice. Loyalty stood over Brittany's body in silence, and a cold feeling came over her. Loyalty wiped the gun off with her dirty shirt, leaving the gun in Brittany's hands. Loyalty set it up to look like a suicide, running out the warehouse leaving Brittany and the now deceased baby in cold blood. Loyalty ran, never looking back, seeing a nearby hotel to use the phone.

The phone rang. "Chanel?" Loyalty was so relieved to hear her friend's voice.

"Oh My God, Loyalty are you OK?" Chanel asked, getting out of bed.

"Yes, at the Westin Hotel, in Ontario," Loyalty told Chanel, looking around and making sure she wasn't being watched.

"OK, on the way," Chanel didn't even finish the sentence before hanging up and rushing out the door.

Moments later, Chanel saw Loyalty standing outside in front of valet. Chanel saw that there was blood on Loyalty's clothes. Loyalty was not in the mood to talk—losing her sister and niece or nephew made her feel uneasy. *Creme lied the whole time, and yet I still have slight feelings for him,* Loyalty thought approaching the car.

"Hey, Girl," Chanel welcomed Loyalty with open arms. Loyalty was in a shock.

"Girl, just wanted some rest for a rough couple of days," Loyalty explained, placing her hand over her forehead in frustration.

"OK, I will take you home," Chanel told Loyalty in a loving manner.

"Hell no," Loyalty said aggressively. "Can't go there now, have to crash at your place until things calm down," Loyalty explained, then looking out the window.

"What is going on?" Chanel asked in concern.

"We will talk," Loyalty told her, still looking out the window.

"Hey, are you serious? It's been three days; you have blood on your shirt," Chanel said, tired of Loyalty's secrets.

"Chanel, just know that I'm fine," Loyalty said, rolling down the window.

"Grandma Joy and I went to fill out a missing person report for you," Chanel explained, pushing her hair back from the wind.

Finally, at Chanel's house, Loyalty couldn't wait any longer for a bath. *My sister tried to kill me, and then Creme—somebody that I made love to—betrayed and set me up for his own personal gain. We not done yet.*

CHAPTER 15:

SINK OR SWIM

Pulling up to the warehouse, Creme was hoping Brittany didn't do anything stupid to Loyalty. Reese and Malo followed behind Creme as they stepped out of the 2016 Chevrolet Tahoe, walking towards rusted metal doors. Creme couldn't believe what he saw walking deeper into the warehouse: Loyalty was no longer tied. Creme, walking past the bathroom, saw Brittany laying on the nasty floor...dead.

"Man, what the fuck? How that bitch get out that tape?" Reese shouted out, confused.

"Nigga, chill out. We have to go," Creme demanded, rushing out, feeling disappointed about everything. Thinking to himself, leaving the warehouse: *I'm still in love with Loyalty even though what I have done to her. Loyalty would of course reject me,* Creme thought.

In the car, the fellas sat for a moment in silence, all shocked that Loyalty actually shot her sister. Creme put gasoline around the building, took a cloth out his Nike joggers, pulled out a piece of cloth, lit it on fire, then tossed it quickly, hurrying back into the truck. He picked up his phone to call Loyalty to see if she would answer. It went straight to the voicemail. Looking out the black tinted window, Creme eventually drove off.

Why couldn't I just be real with both of them? Creme thought. That question would always run around his mind. Creme's anxiety started to mess with his thoughts while driving the boys back to the crib.

* * *

Chanel went over to Loyalty's house to grab her some clothes and her cell phone. Loyalty appreciated Chanel so much, laying on Chanel's fluffy blanket on the couch, trying to avoid laying on her face. Loyalty was still in pain from the blows. She picked up the remote to the fifty-inch TV, turning to the Channel 19 News.

"Nineteen-year-old Brittany Monroe was found dead downtown Cleveland in an abandoned warehouse. Early this morning, a fire was started, leaving poor Brittany and her unborn baby fighting for their lives. Brittany was nine months pregnant...more details on this story shortly. Stayed tuned," the news reporter lady said.

Pressing the off button to the remote with a complete attitude, Loyalty couldn't believe the position she was placed in, and then wondered if it was Creme who started that fire.

"If the world only knew Brittany tried to kill me and had kidnapped me hours ago. Motherfuckers wouldn't give a fuck!" Loyalty spoke to herself, sitting up on the couch. Starting to feel the baby move calmed Loyalty down from her rage. Only five months ago, but it felt like eight already. She reached over for the phone sitting on the marble living room table to give Grandma Joy a call. As the phone rang, she began to get nervous on what to say first to Grandma.

"Hi you have reached Joy, leave a message. God bless," Grandma Joy's machine came on. Loyalty sat puzzled on the couch, with a weird feeling in the bottom of her stomach, not being able to call out. The sudden awareness that Grandma Joy knew Chanel house number, she dialed her number back with no reply again. It made her feel overwhelmed, so she decided to give Chanel a call.

"Hello," Chanel spoke into the phone.

"Wasup, Girl? Call Mama for me and call right back. It's important," Loyalty said, talking fast then hanging up the phone not waiting for a reply from Chanel. While pacing the living room floor back and forth, Chanel finally called her back.

"Hello," Loyalty answered anxiously.

"No answer, Loyalty. You hear that shit about you sister?" Chanel looked at the phone, noticing Loyalty hung up on her. "Well OK," Chanel said while putting her phone down on the passenger seat on the way back home.

Loyalty was still pacing back and forth, because one thing was for certain: Grandma Joy always answered. Grandma didn't have a car to travel. Loyalty and Brittany were the only people Grandma Joy depended on. Loyalty thought of all this, feeling sick, walking to the kitchen to pour a glass of water. She started putting on her Givenchy shoes and thought about calling a taxi until she saw Chanel pull in the driveway.

"Finally!" Loyalty yelled, speed walking out the door to Chanel.

"Here go your clothes, Girl," Chanel said, handing Loyalty her stuff.

"OK, let me use your car?" Loyalty asked while taking the keys out of Chanel's hands. "Thanks, Girl," Loyalty said, getting in the car. Looking in the bag for her phone, she saw one hundred missed calls and sixty messages. She didn't even bother to look, put the car in drive, and drove quickly to check on Grandma Joy.

Grandma Joy stayed not too far from Chanel. Fifteen minutes later, her house appeared to have no lights on. Parking the car in the driveway, she left the car running, and rushed over to the front door. Four minutes had gone by already, and she had been knocking and kicking on the door. Loyalty had tears coming down her face, feeling frustrated. She fell to the floor, not understanding what was going on.

"Where is Mama?" Loyalty cried out, with her knees on the ground. Loyalty was still lost and very hormonal. She got up, looking at the house, then got in the car to leave back to Chanel's house.

Loyalty had no idea that Grandma was on her side, dead on her kitchen floor for hours, from heart failure. Joy couldn't take losing Brittany; it stressed her out completely. Immediately. Loyalty had yet to find out.

On her way back to Chanel's house, Loyalty was pissed, with a displeasure of life at the moment.

"You OK?" Chanel asked Loyalty, looking concerned.

"Can't find Mama," Loyalty spoke, sounding bitter. Chanel let Loyalty know that she spoke with Grandma Joy yesterday. Chanel was standing with her hand glued to her hip. "Well, she is not picking up the phone nor did she open the door. The house pitch black...where is she? Like damn!" Loyalty said, trying not to get upset, standing up, and holding her head in her hands.

Chanel picked up her cell phone. "I'm calling the police."

As Chanel sat in the living room waiting for the police to arrive to make the police report, Loyalty came back inside Chanel's house. Loyalty told Chanel a lie that she was tired and drained, going inside Chanel's room to lay down because she was feeling sleepy. She was really trying to avoid the police all together, but indeed was very worried about Grandma Joy.

I'm pregnant and just killed someone who was my sister. I don't know if Grandma may be ignoring me or what. The man I loved madly, lied to me, Loyalty thought as she laid on Chanel's queen-sized bed, with purple Ralph Lauren blankets.

Loyalty's head began to hurt, and her heart began to feel numb. *I'm totally giving up on love; this baby won't make anything better,* Loyalty thought, looking at the ceiling and questioning her ability to be a mother. *Too late for abortions,* she thought, walking inside Chanel's master bathroom. In the room, she shut the door to hide herself.

There was a knock on the door. "Loyalty, police just left. On the way over to Mama Joy house to see what's going," Chanel said, entering the room out of breath. "Grandma Joy probably slept heavy, or was in the middle of praying," Chanel spoke with concern for her best friend, standing outside the bathroom door with her ear up against the door.

Chanel walked away from the door feeling bad for Loyalty. Chanel hoped Mama was OK. Chanel tried calling a few more times: no answer.

* * *

Hours passed and Loyalty was still in the bathroom on Chanel's floor with bottled emotions, even thoughts of kissing and holding Cream right then.

Loyalty thought that being pregnant would be a perfect moment, but it actually turned into a nightmare.

Loyalty began to wonder: *I worked so hard, come so far, now to be considered a murderer.* Loyalty laid there. Tears fell down her face, furiously.

"Loyalty, Baby, we have to talk! It's about Grandma Joy," Chanel was so terrified to share the news with Loyalty. Loyalty heard Chanel knock, and the request to talk from the sound of things, gave Loyalty a bad vibe. Loyalty immediately opened the door, waiting for Chanel's news. Chanel seemed to be crying—her eyes were red. Loyalty knew her best friend inside out.

"OK, spit it out," Loyalty said, impatient, tired of the stalling. Chanel explained that Mama had been passed away for hours.

"Loyalty, they found her on the kitchen floor dead," Chanel shouted as a tear fell from her smooth face. Loyalty just walked back into the bathroom backwards with a blank look, slamming the door. Loyalty was on the floor, rocking back and forth, and then laid back down until she was falling asleep. Loyalty's nerves were shocked; she felt no longer stable to take care of the baby.

The next morning, feeling like shit, she decided to lay in the shower just so the water drops could somehow caress her body. Loyalty undressed in the shower and wanted nothing but to be zoned out...even from herself.

Loyalty started to feel guilty and ashamed for letting Grandma Joy down. "Grandma Joy won't even be able to see my child born," Loyalty expressed out loud, as tears flowed.

As she sat like a mummy in the tub, she thought about her grandmother losing her life and not being able to help her. Brittany was Loyalty's only sister, and now her blood was on her hands forever.

Loyalty cried. The phone rang. Looking at the phone it read *Devin*. She couldn't believe he even called. "FUCKING BITCH!" Loyalty yelled before putting her phone down.

Creme kept calling. He called again. *I will pick up only to hear him talk, and me be quiet,* Loyalty decided. Loyalty put Dove soap on her body as she watched the phone vibrate again on the toilet. Loyalty still cared for Cream deeply, even though he tore her family apart. The phone rang. Creme answered.

"Hello...hello...hello," Creme sounded genuine. "I love you, no matter what you believe." Loyalty just rolled her eyes listening, after hanging up.

Oh, the nigga got his nerve, set me up, got Brittany pregnant—which by the way is the worst of it all, Loyalty thought as she rinsed the soap off her body before standing up to shut the water off. *He loves me, huh?* Loyalty laughed to herself while grabbing the dry towel from the wall.

Let's see what kind of shirts my girl got, Loyalty thought, searching through Chanel's drawer. Chanel had been very supportive, even giving her space. Chanel was a second-grade teacher at Shaker Heights elementary—she had been there about a year. Loyalty came across a plain black Levi shirt. *Perfect,* Loyalty thought, walking into the kitchen Chanel had cleaned up. Loyalty just decided to make a bowl of Lucky Charms and then watch a little TV.

She turned the TV down to make a call at the job. "Yes, hello. This is Alsadi Monroe, just calling to verify not returning until next week."

The paralegal assistant responded, "I will be sure to let Mr. White get your message, Ms. Monroe. Thank you."

"Cool," Loyalty spoke, as she sat the phone down on the table, hanging up.

Creme continued to call her phone. Loyalty watched the phone ring over and over again. She thought about Monica's *So Gone* song, and couldn't believe that he was the man she was carrying a baby for. *He or she would be brought into this nasty, trifling world,* Loyalty thought, shaking her head in disbelief, still on the couch trying to relax. *What am I going to tell the baby about Brittany once born?* Loyalty thought.

The phone rang, and Loyalty wiped a tear from her pale face.

Cream stopped to look at the phone, then put it back to his ear. "Listen, Baby..." Loyalty hung up.

Honestly, as much as us creating a family together would have been beautiful, it's time for things to start getting ugly, Loyalty thought. She sat up, rubbing her hands together. *Devin lied to me, led me on. Everything about him started to make me feel sick, literally,* she thought, looking into the bathroom mirror. *I once loved that man with every fiber,* Loyalty pointed at the reflection at herself, with tears. *Creme betrayed me, just like my only baby sister!* Loyalty walked out the bathroom, feeling somewhat different about everything. Even her pregnancy.

CHAPTER 16:

ALL-IN

Creme spent days calling Loyalty, trying to get back into her life. It felt like she was already gone. He counted money on the floor of his bedroom. *Life goes on regardless. I'm praying constantly that our baby will be healthy everyday he or she grows. Not mad at Loyalty for doing what she had to do,* Creme was in deep thought. Loyalty had always been there—the little time knowing her. Creme looked through his drawer for one of his jogging fits to put on. The last drawer had his Beretta M9 and a Beretta 93r.

Leaving the house, he jumped into the whip to head over Reese and Malo's house. Minutes later, he arrived at the apartment building to talk to the fellas about the dumb shit that happened days ago with Brittany. One knock at the door, and Reese opened the door.

"Wasup, Nigga?" Reese said, shaking Creme's hand.

"Wasup?" Creme walked inside the door to stand in the living room, feeling somewhat shocked about all the shit that went down. "Listen, Nigga," Creme said, still standing with his hands in his jacket pockets, ready to get a few things off his chest.

"Yeah, that hoe was tweaking," Malo said as he stood with his arms folded.

"All this shit was hot from the beginning, drip failed period," Reese explained while he counted his money.

Devin rubbed his chain in deep thought from conversation. "Let's just keep grinding. I deserve all the dust Loyalty blowing at me." Devin sat down on the plush blue sofa.

Sarcastically, Reese said, "Nigga, just fuck her and get on shit. Dick is magic, remember that shit!" They all laughed.

75

Devin continued to stay sitting as his thoughts drifted, feeling a bit emotional about losing Loyalty. Creme knew he fucked up. He walked to the bathroom, closed the door, and contemplated calling her. *Miss Loyalty voice, body...shit every piece of her that made me truly understand the man I really am. Shit, maybe I'm a monster!* Devin looked in the mirror before taking his phone out his hoodie pocket to face the woman he betrayed and tried to leave for dead.

The phone rang. Loyalty answered, just breathing into the phone. Creme took over the conversation as usual. "Can we just talk, please?" Devin tried to plead with Loyalty, but she did not budge. "I know you not gone speak back but I love you always will, Baby. I fucked up and have no problem admitting that to you constantly," Devin continued. "Had time to think things through, Loyalty, going to let you breathe, give you space. I love ... " Loyalty interrupted before hanging up.

"Love you, too," Loyalty said, and then hung up.

Loyalty sat in the living room covered in a thick pink blanket. She couldn't believe Devin really had her heart torn apart. A tear dropped down Loyalty's face, and she quickly wiped it because Chanel was calling. Loyalty had promised Chanel she would stop stressing and really try to enjoy her pregnancy.

The phone rang. Chanel spoke enthusiastically into the phone. "Hey, you ready for Mama Joy funeral yet?"

Loyalty spoke up, feeling so torn apart. "No, not going. Can't bear to see Grandma Joy like that. I'll take good memories with me," Loyalty said, laying still with her eyes glued to the TV.

"OK, here if you need anything. Here for ya," Chanel said, sad about Loyalty's response.

"OK, thank you so much, Chanel."

"Love and adore you."

"The feeling is mutual, Best Friend. Love you longtime ... like the Chinese folks," Loyalty joked. They both laughed then hung up.

* * *

Brittany was always on Loyalty's mind. Loyalty picked up a magazine to scan through. *Why was she so mad at me, and even tried harming me?* Loyalty sat there all-in thoughts, starting to think that all along Brittany knew about Loyalty being pregnant. *Why would she even mention it?* Finally, home in bed, it had been about a good month since the kidnapping. Loyalty changed the house code to the gates of the complex.

She sat on the couch laughing watching *Love & Hip Hop*. Loyalty loved Masika, thought she dressed so fly, and talked very intelligent. The phone rang. Loyalty let the phone ring twice before answering.

"Hello?" No one said anything. Loyalty looked at her phone again, and then repeated herself.

"Wasup?" a very familiar voice said. Loyalty's heart began pounding faster, and her knees buckled.

"What do you want, Devin?" Loyalty said in a soft voice, but still slightly upset.

"Can we talk for a moment? Can I come over?" he asked desperately.

"Um, no you cannot, kidnapper," Loyalty say honestly.

"Chill with that shit," Devin said, feeling terrible. "Nothing bad was gonna happen to you."

"Really? Bad shit already happened," Loyalty reminded him. Devin was furious about Loyalty's comments, so he hung up.

As Creme exited the bathroom and went back into the bar, he thought of everything. Loyalty's words actually made him nervous. He did not believe that he could actually lose Loyalty. *I just wanted her to forgive me so we can raise our beautiful child together,* Creme thought as he walked over to the bar.

"Let me get some Henny and Coca Cola," he said to the waitress, gently. He swallowed his cup, tired of getting nowhere with Loyalty. *Whatever.* Creme threw his hands up. Reese and Malo decided to come out that night to The Alibi, and all the bitches were on them. They loved it.

See, Creme was used to that, yet all he could think of was Ms. Monroe. Loyalty was so special to him: young, and motivated. A couple of the girls that worked for him came over to the bar, and then started dancing seductively around them, taking their clothes off piece by piece. Big ass, tits, and booty.

Creme just sat there, smiling, shaking his head. Creme and the guys threw at least ten bands on them. He turned around and Malo was getting some head by one of the dancers named Crystal. Shit was lit. A couple minutes after, he dapped up the fellas, and then left the club, ready for bed.

* * *

Fifteen minutes later, pulling in the driveway to park, Creme was walking in the house tired, with a tote load of shit on my mind. He was feeling hungry and pulled some broccoli and rice out and cut up some veggies. *Loyalty always made me something with some sort of vegetables to give me some extra strength,* Creme smiled to himself.

After eating and getting ready for bed, Creme's phone rang. It said *Alsadi.* Creme got a bit nervous and did not know what to do but to ignore the call he had been waiting for, for what felt like forever. *I'm going through shit,* Creme told himself, trying to figure out how to handle all this shit. *I'll call her back.* Devin put the phone back on the nightstand. Devin's phone rang again. It read *Alsadi* again, so he picked up this time.

"Hey, Baby," Creme, spoke feeling like a big kid again.

"Listen, our baby is due in three months. December fifteen," Loyalty explained with frustration in her voice.

"OK, My Love," Creme said, rubbing his forehead before laying back on his pillow.

"Great, so is that all, Devin?" Loyalty asked, while looking at her gel nails.

"Yes. Know that I love you, always will people fuck up, forgive me, My Love," Creme said again, pleading to Loyalty for forgiveness.

"I do," Loyalty said, now sounding a bit calmer. "Take care of your responsibility, Devin, and we are even, Baby. Point blank."

"Cool, will do. That's a promise," Creme expressed easily. Creme wanted to be there. *But why?*

They both ended the call.

Loyalty laid there on her canopy bed wrapped in Ralph Lauren blankets, thinking of all the chaos. Loyalty couldn't believe through all this she was pregnant. *My feelings are everywhere*, Loyalty thought. *Am scared, but happy at the same time. Me and Devin first child seemed amazing at first.* She drifted to sleep to dream of Brittany killing her baby…

* * *

Devin had so much going, but nothing real flowing. Alsadi made him feel free: aware. He missed Loyalty dearly. The efforts were thin though. Devin knew he couldn't stand a chance being back with Alsadi, after he finished texting a few chicks he then drifted to sleep.

Devin woke up the next morning feeling energized, brushed his teeth, put on his black Nike outfit with some all-black Airs, and left out the house feeling like a better man for himself and child. He came outside to straight grind. Put up some better light fixtures in front of the clubs Alibi and Naked, and then sent some checks off from his payroll.

Life was cool, it just got lonely sometimes. *Any bitch can have this body if she is lucky; no bitch can have my time. I'm picky, strict rules with the dick,* Creme laughed to himself. Alsadi would make life so much happier, but it was just how shit had to go, so he had to accept that.

The phone rang.

"Wasup, Ugly Nigga?" Malo said.

"Nigga, wasup?" Creme said, laughing.

"Slide through for a few. Want to explain this drip," Malo said.

"Alright, be on my way in twenty minutes. Leaving Club Naked," Creme said, and then hung up.

Not hitting no drips, Creme thought to himself while on his way to meet with the guys. *I'm good. Have enough of my own money for right now.* He scrolled through his phone, looking at pics of him and Alsadi.

CHAPTER 17:

NOT HER

Loyalty woke up at six-thirty a.m. on Thursday morning, feeling unsure about everything. Even work. She couldn't bare having people look at her or even asking her questions. She had to do something, because she was tired of feeling bad for herself. She was already seven months pregnant; Brittany's baby would have been two months now. Two months now.

Walking into her marble black tiled bathroom, she stood in front of the mirror and looked at the reflection. It seemed as though she was staring at a monster.

Murdered Brittany. Shot her twice in the head with no remorse, Loyalty began to cry to the soft music of Brian Culbertson. *Lights Off* started to play in her head. *Murdered my sister, Grandma Joy is gone, my love betrayed me in the worst way imaginable.* She turned the shower knobs on to take a long quiet shower; Loyalty's body just fell slowly to the floor, sitting on the big furry rug that Brittany had bought for her months ago. She missed Brittany so much. *She was carrying my only nephew.* As she was taking off her clothes, the phone rang. It was Chanel.

"Hey, checking on my big girl!" Chanel said, laughing.

Loyalty smiled a little. "Thanks. Taking every day one step at a time. Just about to take a shower."

"Make sure you pray and eat healthy," Chanel said. "About to head to work, check on you later. Love ya!"

"Love you, too!"

After her shower, Loyalty put some clothes on: a nude pencil skirt with a white top and black blazer. She slid on her Chanel shoes, drank a cup of mimosa, then headed out. She felt bad for drinking, but just felt so under pressure. Leaving her driveway, she also started to hope that no fingerprints would come back from the warehouse. Loyalty felt frantic—she could lose everything: career, house, and car worst all...her child. Tears fell from her mascara eyes. Trying to keep it together...Loyalty just couldn't. She grabbed some napkins from her YSL purse that sat in the passenger seat. *I couldn't bear losing my first child, and how could Devin do this to me?*

Loyalty arrived to work ten minutes early, as always, before pulling herself together. She just got back to business. Loyalty sat in court listening to a trial. Loyalty had flashbacks of Brittany opening the door then Loyalty shooting Brittany twice. Loyalty jumped as Bailiff Cory Sanders leaned over to ask something.

"Hey, you OK, Alsadi?" Bailiff Corey asked, looking concerned. Loyalty continued to fix the paperwork.

Many hours passed, and court was finally over for Loyalty, so she was on the way back to the office to catch up on emails, straighten up a little, and look over some cases since she had not been there for weeks. Loyalty came across a photo of Grandma Joy and Brittany.

With two more hours of work left, Loyalty's feet were hurting, and she was craving something to eat. Loyalty told her doctor that she and Devin would be married already. Loyalty started holding on to her stomach—she was in pain.

"Let me get some water," she said to herself. Loyalty opened her mini fridge, then grabbed a mini water.

* * *

Devin was at the trap house for three days—hell of money made, that's facts! Creme had to make a drop later and was exhausted from all the hectic events that transpired with Brittany and Loyalty. Creme had to keep going regardless. Bagging up over one hundred thousand dollars in dope in a garbage bag, he tossed the garbage bag in a Jordan fitness bag. Before leaving, Creme looked out all the windows and rushed to the 2017 Lexus, going to the back seat to stuff the bag under a secret compartment. Creme's stash spot made a perfect room: no one would ever think. Creme smiled to himself: *smart MUTHA Fucka*. Locking the secret compartment, Creme went into the house to put money up. He chilled for an hour before leaving out, just to let shit slow down. It was still early in the day—around five p.m. He picked up the phone to call Reese.

"Salute, Brah," Reese said, grinning through the phone.

"Salute! Making money!" Creme said, aggressively. "How shit been up there?"

"Everything good. Money flowing. Chickens paying like they weigh," Reese said.

"Good news, Nigga. That's what I like to hear for real for real. Just checking your pulse though. You be safe."

They both hung up.

All this wild shit that's been happening in the last two months, police and news haven't brought up anything about Brittany's death. Only that Brittany and the baby were set on fire at the Warehouse, Creme thought. *Everything was too late.* Creme was burying his head inside his hands, feeling somewhat sorry for himself.

Creme got his shit together, standing up at the neon marble chair, He had to get over the shit ASAP. Creme grabbed the car keys to the Lexus—his head got to bothering him again for some reason. Anxiety! On the way to the building, Creme was ready to get rid of this new shit and wanted to ditch the car after his dropoff.

Creme put a CD inside the radio, and NBA Youngboy blasted through the speakers, Hold Me Down. Instantly, he was thinking about Alsadi. *My peach, my love.* Creme would always have love for Loyalty; she would always be in his heart, he though, with a huge smile across his face.

He checked under the seat for his Glock 345, a couple minutes from pulling up to the building. He was anxious to get this shit off. Parking on the side of the building, he sat for a few minutes. All of sudden, Creme noticed a black Charger pull up behind his car very slowly. Three white men came out with much force.

"Get out of the car!" one police officer responded, with tats all over his face. Creme slowly exited the vehicle with his hands on his head. An officer with black hair, grey eyes, and a heavy built body then read Creme his rights, forcing him to turn around.

"What the fuck y'all doin, ain't did shit!" he was upset, yelling at the officers. Creme spoke furious, as he was being placed in handcuffs. "Get this shit off!" Crème continued to argue with the cops.

The officer with the tats told him to shut up before he wore the toe tag instead. Creme shook his head, disgusted. He looked out the window in the opposite direction. The smart mouth officer walked Creme to the all-black Dodge Charger, and told Creme, "Watch yo head," as he was getting in the squad car.

The officer told other officers that Devin had three open warrants, and three more vice cars pulled up. One car had a dog. Creme dropped his head, sitting in the backseat and just knew it was over: his house, cars, all the money, even his clubs...gone. He knew that he might not even see his child born. Creme thought this in anger and frustration. Creme shed a tear then lifted his head back up. "Fuck it," Creme said as the car pulled off, headed straight to the police department.

* * *

Alsadi, on the way home, ordered some Taco Costo from Downtown Cleveland in the flats. Finishing work, Loyalty arrived at the house door, ready to just fall asleep. Loyalty placed the food and her purse on the round glass table, walking in the room to change into something very comfortable. The phone kept ringing over and over; Loyalty walked back in the kitchen, looking inside her purse. The phone read a weird number; Loyalty noticed. She usually wouldn't answer, but this time, Loyalty picked up.

Alsadi said, "Hello?"

Devin said, "Don't hang up."

"What do want?" Loyalty asked, eager to hear Devin's response.

"Listen, I'm in the county jail right now, Loyalty. I might not be able to see our child be born," he stated, feeling upset.

Alsadi sat on the phone in silence, in pure confusion. Sad. Regretful.

"My Love?" Devin asked.

"Cut that shit out, OK? I don't know what to say. Good luck or whatever," Loyalty said, fed up and angry.

"Just be here. Love you, My Dear..."

"Sixty seconds remaining," said the county voice.

Alsadi hung up. She couldn't believe Devin's words; everything was really over, Alsadi thought while sitting in the chair. Loyalty looked at the phone to call Chanel.

"Hey, Love," Chanel said.

"Hey. Calling to ask you a few questions, OK?"

"Yes, whatever you like," Chanel said, happy to hear from Loyalty.

"Cool. If anything was to ever happen, want you to take care of the baby."

Chanel was confused. "What are you talking about? Why wouldn't you be here for the baby?"

"Understand that you will always be my sister, so let me ask you this one thing? Raise the baby to be smart, brave, educated, OK?" Loyalty stated, being stern and honest.

Chanel was crying. "I don't understand! I will do everything for you, Loyalty. Going to raise little pumpkin to love you deeply."

"Love you forever," Loyalty said, and pushed the end button.

Loyalty's thoughts raced. She was tired and hurt by everything. Devin was out of her life, and she even started to regret letting him in. Standing at the sink, she made a glass of water, and then decided to lay down for bed.

Hearing a loud sound: "Put your hands up now! Get on the floor!" a group of police shouted—ten officers were in her room. "You're being arrested for the murder of Brittany Monroe," an officer stated. One officer with tats all on his face read Loyalty her rights. Four officers lifted her out of bed and escorted her out of the house.

CHAPTER 18:

JUICE

On October the tenth, of 2016, looking in the judge's eyes, the judge didn't look like she would take it easy on Loyalty. "Name is Judge Sperry; may everyone take a seat."

The courtroom was so packed; even Chanel called off work and showed up, loving Chanel. Loyalty stood in an orange jumpsuit, hands and feet shackled. Loyalty was embarrassed; the bailiffs and prosecutors knew Loyalty personally.

"We have Ms. Alsadi Monroe, a twenty-two-year-old full-time paralegal...for this company. Correct?" Judge Sperry was talking to Mr. Lopez, Alsadi's lawyer.

"Yes, that is correct," Mark Lopez responded in confidence. "Ms. Monroe has also been with this company for two years and is a valuable employee here at the Justice Center."

Prosecutor Maria Gomez interrupted: "Excuse me, Your Honor," the Prosecutor said in disbelief, tired of Alsadi's lawyer rambling on. "This lady murdered and tortured Brittany Monroe. Alsadi's actions are unforgivable."

An hour into the case, Loyalty was feeling sick. Mr. Lopez was pretty good at his job. *Paid his ass about twenty thousand,* Loyalty thought.

Ms. Gomez carried on saying that, "Alsadi's fingerprints from the gunshot residue verified that she had everything to do with the passing of Brittany Monroe passing," Gomez started with aggression, using her hands actively.

The judge then called a quick recess, a break lasting only for about thirty minutes. Judge Kelly Sperry came into the room sitting in her chair with her blonde hair, brown eyes, and on-and-off attitude. "So, we are going to proceed with this case for October twenty-second, twenty-sixteen for Ms. Monroe in this case of Brittany Monroe." The bailiffs walked towards Loyalty looking so aggressive and careless. The officers grabbed Loyalty, walking her back to the holding cell. Loyalty, leaving the courtroom, waved at Chanel before becoming invisible again behind tall walls. Chanel was Loyalty's comfort.

Loyalty shared a room with a gang member named Curry, a pretty cool girl at five-six, one hundred forty pounds, dark skin, and freckles, pretty teeth...a pretty girl. Laying on the bottom bunk, she thought of times she shared with Devin. Devin meant so much to Loyalty, yet Loyalty hated Devin at the same time.

Loyalty curled her body into a fetal position, confused, lonely, and misunderstood. Yes, Loyalty telling the real story would have been easier for her, but no one got it. So, Loyalty taking the fall for everything didn't matter because either way her family was gone.

* * *

Almost seven months pregnant, in jail, Loyalty lost her position as a paralegal and everything else she worked hard for.

"Girl, why you crying?" Curry asked Loyalty, looking to help.

"Nothing. I'm OK," Loyalty told Curry, while pacing the small cell. Loyalty wiped some tears from the side of her puffy face. Loyalty was a super nerd and knew how to carry herself swiftly, and also stand tall like a hood chick.

Loyalty always—for some reason—showed her good side around Devin. Loyalty chose to do more with her life: going to college and chasing real things to be different.

Curry carried on: "Any bitch can get it, if you call, Loyalty," Curry said aggressively, but serious. Alsadi laughed.

"Thanks, Curry. Cool, Mama."

Curry was really a stud but looked pretty with tats everywhere. Straight bully. Every girl was scared of Curry, but of course...not Loyalty, Curry immediately took a liking to Loyalty. Loyalty let Curry know early on that she didn't do cat. Curry understood Loyalty, closing eyes, and hoping the lawyer would be able to convince the judge not to give her too much time...even though he never gave Loyalty full intel on the truth. It seemed like appearing remorseful didn't work, and everything was just Loyalty's karma.

At the end of the day, Loyalty was going to accept her time, and lay low. Loyalty was worried about her dear child. Even knowing that Chanel would take perfect care of the baby, Loyalty still worried terribly.

Hearing loud noises throughout the cells, loud talking, smoking weed, and doing other drugs, Loyalty on her bunk turned to the wall feeling so uncomfortable. She just rested her eyelids.

* * *

"Man, what the fuck?" Loyalty shouted, jumping up from the thin sheet, waking up to the guards banging on the bars with their billy clubs. Loyalty was angry because she needed more sleep. It was around six a.m.

"Curry, Monroe, let's go! Time for chow," the correctional officer demanded, opening the metal door. Both of the ladies got up from the dusty bunks to brush their teeth. Loyalty got to the cafeteria feeling cold and unwanted. Grabbing the food, Loyalty sat down right next to Curry.

She caught this girl staring at her. Brushing the weird eye contact off, she thought, *that bitch deserved to die, speaking so angry across from us a couple tables over but not too far.* Curry explained to Loyalty that the girl had life in prison, and the chick didn't care about anything...not even the guards. Obviously, the lady had nothing to lose. She was Mexican, fat, sloppy, and built with buck teeth. Everyone called her Foxy. She was around forty years old.

Loyalty finished eating, and then walked back to the pod to make a phone call.

"How you doin, Baby?" Loyalty talked proudly.

"I'm cool, just constantly worrying about you, Dear Friend. How is the baby?" Chanel asked.

"The baby is so far along. Chanel, you get everything you might need for the baby? Don't forget I need lots of pics," Loyalty asked Chanel nicely, holding tight to the jail phone.

"No problem. Loyalty?"

"Yes, Dear?" she was tired, but aware of Chanel's words.

"Did you have anything to do with your sister's murder?" she asked, scared but concerned.

Alisadi hung up the phone.

* * *

Chanel woke up the next morning, excited to start her new job as a ninth-grade teacher. She had just been hired, days ago. Chanel fixed her hair in a bun. She was wearing a white button-down with a bow tie, black fitted jeans, and Chanel's shoes were red.

Chanel walking into Maple Heights High School, big. All the students—well, most of them that came—made contact with Chanel in the hallways. The children seemed interesting and eager to learn, Chanel believed.

Chanel walked to the second floor of her new classroom and was very bubbly. Even though she had been a teacher before, teaching young adults' kind of made her a little nervous. Entering classroom 2018, the room had huge walls with different colored tables in front of one another, sitting against a blue wall. Chanel's desk was rectangle shaped and brown, left with a red apple, some pencils, chalk, and a new Apple laptop the school had given to Chanel as a gift, which she thought was super sweet.

As students began to enter the room, picking up the yellow chalk that was left on the desk, Chanel wrote her name across the board so the students would notice. "My name is Ms. Lauren," she explained with a graceful smile across her face. All the children seemed respectful so far, and a few of the children even asked a couple questions to help get to know them all before beginning class.

"You look so fine," a student ranted while looking her up and down. Chanel looked at the boy.

"Seriously?" she asked, while walking closer to him. "What may your name be, sir?" Chanel asked in a stern voice.

"Jerome," he replied, rubbing his chin, slouching in his chair, and seeming to be bothered.

"Well, Jerome, you will never talk to me like that again or you will be removed from this class." Chanel pointed at the door. She felt eager and confident to teach her new class, even though there was a little hiccup.

Hours passed, the bell rang, and the students stood up, giving Chanel all of the assignments, they had worked on early throughout the day about the trees and oxygen. Chanel met all students at the door to collect the papers.

Her phone rang.

"Mark Lopez, speaking!"

"Yes, hello. How you doing, Mark?" It was Alsadi's lawyer.

"Hi, I'm calling you, Ms. Lauren, to go over a few concerns about Ms. Monroe's case. The judge is looking to give Alsadi fifteen to twenty years. Ten maybe with good behavior, totally understanding that Alsadi is pregnant and due any moment." Chanel was trying her hardest to get Loyalty home early with the baby. "Who will be caring for the child once it's born?" Mark asked Chanel, concerned.

Chanel was in shock and got up from the desk holding her mouth.

"The baby will be with me until Alsadi is released; I'm the guardian of the child," Chanel told Mark, proudly.

CHAPTER 19:

SHEEP & WOLVES

Loyalty had been sleeping all day, and couldn't do much but sleep, read, and eat. Loyalty was growing so tired of it, and hoping to get her old life back, so badly. She got up to use the phone to check on Chanel—Chanel was such a true friend, and Loyalty was so thankful every day for Chanel's patience. She put through the collect call.

"Hey, how you doin today?" Chanel asked, sounding bittersweet.

Alsadi responded. "Keeping my head. The baby is always bouncing on Loyalty bladder; not getting any decent sleep around here," she laughed, rubbing her round belly.

Chanel continued. "Look, Alsadi, your lawyer called earlier today with some news. He said the judge may be looking to give you fifteen to twenty years if found guilty. Ten maybe with good behavior."

"Wow," Loyalty said, pulling her hair from her face in disbelief. Loyalty's head fell to the floor, and her eyes wandered. "Sorry, Chanel, for bringing all this stress and baggage."

"I promise to do better. Started a new job, when you have the baby in two months, will have plenty of time to spend with him or her before, depending on daycare," Chanel said.

Alsadi interrupted Chanel. "Chanel, no daycares!" Loyalty said, speaking serious and irritated. "I'm not willing to have no one around the baby but you."

"Sixty seconds remaining on this call," the operator spoke into the phone.

"Promise," Loyalty continued.

"I have to work, Loyalty," Chanel said, feeling all over the place.

"Please promise me," Alsadi said.

"Promise," Chanel replied.

"Love you so much. Give you a call tomorrow." Loyalty hung up the phone quickly.

Chanel left the classroom, feeling frustrated and scared. *How could Loyalty have so many demands on my life?* Chanel thought, walking proudly out of the school with red high heels on. Inside her car, Chanel was ready to go home, catch up on some rest, and grade more papers.

Chanel stopped at a local Subway not far from the High School and was so hungry. "Yes, let me have a foot long, white bread, roasted with provolone cheese." The Subway employee asked if there was anything else needed. She told the cashier that was all, and the employee wrapped the sandwich.

Her phone rang. It was Devin. "Wasup, this Creme. This Chanel?"

Chanel looked at the phone in disgust. Chanel couldn't stand Creme; all he brought in Loyalty's life was stress, murder, and betrayal. "Yes, this is Chanel," Chanel said, grabbing her food to leave.

"Let Loyalty know I need my child in my life. She is not stopping that, you hear me?" Devin said, aggressively speaking.

"I'm taking custody of the baby very soon, so that will be left to me, Boo Boo," Chanel told Creme sarcastically, in a protective manner.

"Fuck that shit!" Creme hung up the phone, furious.

* * *

"You have a collect call from Creme."

"Brah, wasup?" Reese was pumped to hear from his brother Creme, sounding about business.

"Need a location," Devin said. "Send you a letter in j pay in a minute."

"Bet." Reese hung up.

* * *

94

Waking up from having a terrible dream of shooting someone, a wetness began to fall down Loyalty's leg, and sharp pains went across the bottom of her belly. Alsadi began to panic, instantly shouting Curry to get up.

"Curry, wake up!" Loyalty was in pain. Curry got off the bunk with force, wiping the cold from out her eyes, worried for Loyalty. Curry didn't have to help at all, but she was willing to. Curry could have ignored Loyalty or anything, but instead Curry grabbed a cloth, and Curry hurried up to wet the cloth with lukewarm water. Curry placed the cloth on Loyalty's head.

"It's ok, Girl. Going to get some help for you. Do you believe that you're going into labor?" Curry asked Loyalty, looking for the first time scared to death.

Alsadi replied, with sweat on her forehead. "Feeling dizzy, having shortness of breath..."

Curry finally got one of the correctional officers to come help, even though he dragged his feet to do so. Being rushed to the hospital to deliver the baby in so much pain, Loyalty couldn't bear it any longer, having trouble breathing the whole ride. Feeling in shock and anxious, she arrived at the Metro Hospital on the west side of Cleveland. The pain began to get closer, and sharper.

Loyalty yelled. "Get me anything for this pain, please!" They offered numbing medicine, but Loyalty later realized something was wrong when the nurse gave her another ultrasound. The nurse expressed that the baby was in fetal distress. Loyalty laid on the uncomfortable hospital bed, looking up at the screen. "What are you talking about? Please don't let anything happen to the baby!" Alsadi said, pleading.

"Definitely will try, Ms. Alsadi," Dr. Love explained in confidence, trying to keep Alsadi calm as possible. "Come on, let's get this baby out. We will be doing a C-section." A nurse ran over to the doctor, who was with another patient explaining.

Alsadi was feeling scared, and alone. She was hoping for the best overall, and that the baby was healthy. About twenty minutes later the baby was out. A beautiful girl, but they heard no crying. The doctor let Loyalty know that the baby was not breathing. Crying hysterically, Loyalty's whole world seemed to be over—really over. The doctors showed the baby to Loyalty. A beautiful baby girl that weighed seven pounds and three ounces.

The baby never opened up her eyes. Alsadi was angry, bitter, and lost. Loyalty laid there broken, empty, and incomplete.

* * *

After spending only, a day at Metro Hospital and then being taken back to the place Loyalty looked at as Green Mile, she was glad she never called Chanel to come to the hospital. It turned out to be a terrible experience for Loyalty. Loyalty planned on giving Chanel a call once she got back and situated.

"You have a collect call from Alsadi."

"Why are you just now calling me? It's been almost two days!" Chanel said, kind of pissed at Loyalty, her pregnant best friend.

"I know..."

"So, what's been up?" Chanel asked, being nosey and frank with Loyalty.

Loyalty was stuttering before actually getting the words out of her mouth. "The baby passed away yesterday morning. Fetal distress. Too late to save the baby," she said, as one tear caressed her caramel cheek.

Chanel instantly cried out, dropping the phone. "Nooo!" Chanel yelled, laying on the floor. "Sorry, Loyalty."

Loyalty wiped her cold cheek. "Chanel be strong. Not just for me, but yourself. All I have is you now, Chanel. My baby will never be able to see my face or smile." Another tear-filled Loyalty eyes, while explaining to Chanel. She wiped her tears off quickly.

Chanel tried to get herself together from the really disappointing news she had just received from someone she cared for so much. "Creme called my phone. He actually was threatening me," she said, wiping her face and trying to explain all the shit weird that was going on in her absence.

"Don't worry, I'll handle that," Loyalty said.

Even though Loyalty loved Creme so much, in her head, shit wouldn't feel better until he was gone completely out her life...for good! Loyalty had changed and betrayal had turned her into a beast.

Loyalty would not sleep until Devin, Creme, was dead.

DEDICATION

God

Julia Jones

Cynthia Edmonds & the Edmonds Family

Aaryan Jones

Brooklyn Childs

Jamar Jones

Zelmon Rubin

Climmie Crawford

Mrs. Maureen Daily

Jameel Davis